CALEB'S TESTIMONY

A Novel

Helen Glowacki

Interior Artwork by Ricky Davis
German Translation by Katharina Leipp
Cover by dr Design and Associates

Novels by Helen Glowacki

When God Broke Grandma's Heart
When God Took Grandma Home
When Grandma Chased the Spirits
The Granddaughter and the Monkey Swing
Grandma's Little Book of Poetry: The Story of God's Plan of Salvation
Abiding Faith, Hidden Treasure
And Then They Asked God
Caleb's Testimony

Why God Why Series by Helen Glowacki

To What Purpose?
Why God Why?
Why Trust Scripture?
What Should I Know About Life after Death And The Coming Tribulation?
What Does God Want Me To Do RIGHT NOW?
Do Our Little Sins *Really* Count?

Other non-fiction Books by Helen Glowacki

Politically Incorrect: The Get Some Gumption Handbook
When Enough is Enough
Overcoming Depression: How to be Happy
What No One Is Telling You about Addictions
****
Authors Website: www.Helenglowacki.com

Face book: http://www.facebook.com/pages/The-Grandmother-Series/155300907853909?ref=ts

CALEB'S TESTIMONY

A Novel

Helen Glowacki

Interior Artwork by Ricky Davis
German Translation by Katharina Leipp
Cover by dr Design and Associates

MISSION STATEMENT

To Serve

God

With All Our Strength

And

All Our Heart

Helen Glowacki

DEDICATION

This book is dedicated to Kathy Leipp whose vivacious personality and loving support for my work has truly touched my heart. Though living miles away, in Mühlacker, Germany, Kathy has become a very special friend and the best "fan" anyone could have. Like me Kathy is also New Apostolic and, as a faithful child of God, works to share her faith with as many souls as possible. Kathy has provided the German translation for this book to help us in our quest to bring testimony outside the United States. Thank you Kathy for all the kindness you have shown me, for all the work you have placed into the translation of this novel, and for your beautiful example of true friendship.

NOTE TO THE READER

The novels by Helen Glowacki are works of fiction. While some events in this novel reflect the expertise and support of those in particular vocations, references to real people, events, organizations, or locales are intended only to provide a sense of authenticity, and are used fictitiously. Characters, incidents and dialogue are drawn from the author's imagination and are not to be construed as real. Any resemblance to actual persons, living or dead is entirely coincidental.

The non-fiction books by Helen Glowacki represent the opinion, research, religious beliefs and scriptural interpretations of the author and not meant to be used in lieu of the advice of ministerial, theological, medical or psychological experts. No part of these books may be used or reproduced in any manner whatsoever without written permission except in the case of brief quotations embodied in critical articles and reviews.

The King James Version (KJV) of the Bible, which is public domain in the United States, is used throughout the books by this author. For further study, the author recommends the New King James Version (NKJV) of the Bible as easier reading and less usage of the old world language while remaining true to the original text.

ACKNOWLEDGEMENTS

Special thanks to Dr. Richard Weiner for correcting my medical description of bilateral knee surgery and for being the inspiration for one of my characters. Thanks to Kim Favole, RN, Thomas Jablonski, LPN, Sierra Harley, CNA, Valerie Evans, CNA, Suze Sulfradin, CNA, Josette Le blanc, CNA and others at Chatsworth @ PGA who willingly give their heart, love and expertise to those in need. Thanks to David Kashuba, Founder of First Rehabilitation, and to his staff, Laurie, Debbie, Narkie, Diana, Pam, Geri, Jack and Hugh, who provided their rehabilitative expertise. Thanks to Ricky Davis, Pretoria North, Gauteng, South Africa for allowing us to use his beautiful sketches at the beginning of every chapter, and to Darren Robinson, dr Design and Associates, West Palm Beach, Florida for his meticulous assembly of the cover. I also owe a great debt to Katharina Leipp, Mühlacker, Germany for translating this novel into the German language.

Special thanks to my husband Wally who provides so much support to my work and makes my computer behave. Thanks to my children and grandchildren for the constancy of their love and encouragement, and to Reverend Herold Ambroise for his fervent prayers. Special thanks to Richard Levinson for providing the first opportunity through which I could develop my writing skills, to my brothers and sisters and ministers in faith who give so freely of their love and prayers, and to my Face Book friends who pray for me and also support this ministry.

But most of all, my heartfelt, humble thanks to our Heavenly Father for His inspiration, guiding hand, protection, and never-ending love. May this work bring joy to His heart and help find that last soul!

"One thing have I desired

of the Lord,

that I will seek after;

that I may dwell

in the house of the Lord

all the days of my life,

to behold the beauty of the Lord,

and to enquire in his temple."

Psalm 27: 4

MESSAGE FROM THE AUTHOR

Most of us wish that God would manifest Himself in some incredibly obvious and indisputable manner so that every doubt is forever washed away. Perhaps our Heavenly Father has the same wish, but if He fulfilled those wishes, Satan could accuse Him of affecting man's free will to choose between good and evil and whether to follow God's statutes or not, thus not fulfill the righteousness under which He has chosen to labor.

Therefore, it is through our personal choices that we grow in faith, that we choose to follow God and thereby learn to recognize that He can and does manifest His power by blessing us and showing us that He is with us. Sadly, many never look for these blessings and may chalk those experiences up to mere coincidence and do not identify them as the godly interventions that they are. But when we *do* look for the blessing, we become aware of the many activities through which God works and which, by simple odds, could not be mere coincidence. We see them as a series of planned circumstances leading to a specific end. We also learn that when God blesses us, He often does this through the people we encounter and therefore who we meet may not be a haphazard or coincidental event either.

Some of these people become role models who influence the direction of our life, others become an inspiration to help us weather the storms we face, and some encourage us when we feel defeated. Others may provide a fleeting yet helping hand or offer a skill we have need of. Some may have a strong faith themselves or may have no faith at all. They may have taught us how to develop more love, learn more appreciation, or grow in faith. Meeting them may be a life changing experience or a gentle nudge, yet are a series of planned and deliberate events. God may have brought them into our life to provide us that which we require and therefore use that circumstance to bless us.

When we look back on our experiences with this in mind, we will most likely recognize a pattern through which our lives were shaped and our paths directed. Accepted as such and viewed from a spiritual point of view, these people and events become a part of the very special experiences which build our faith. In fact, we can discern how even our *negative* experiences and associations play their part in helping direct our path and opening our understanding and, it is through these experiences that we learn the value of striving to spurn the temptations of evil and make the decision to learn God's words and live as He suggests. As we learn God's plan is for us… and look for His blessings, we also allow Him to work in our heart and soul to help us recognize where we need correction and what we still need to learn. We realize that when we feel assured that God is with us, thus trust that He will turn even devastating circumstances into a blessing, we can weather our challenges with greater courage.

None of this however happens overnight. It is a slow process, a learning process where we make the personal decision to believe and we institute the faith required for us to trust God fully. This trust encourages us in our decision to follow God's precepts as described throughout scripture. It helps us recognize when, where, and why God blesses us and how we can become a part of the Bride of Christ.

Whenever we face a problem, it is human nature to want to know what has gone wrong and what we should do. We want to make an educated decision rather than an emotional one. We must understand that knowledge provides self-empowerment and guides us toward asking the right questions and perhaps attempting to find our answers through research. However, while many seek knowledge about a disturbing issue, many do not seek knowledge about God, do not research scripture and therefore shortchange themselves spiritually. Yet, in His love for *all* of mankind, God helps both believers and unbelievers hoping to open their heart to His presence and His love. He desires that we *all* witness His work in our lives and that we *all* turn to Him in trust. But unless we open our heart, learn of God and recognize the blessing, we struggle with our concerns.

Interestingly, many studies have been conducted which demonstrate that prayer carries an incredible amount of power. Prayer is a form of communication. Proper communication in every phase of our life is incredibly important, yet sadly, many people have trouble communicating properly. When we cannot convey what we are experiencing, what worries fill our heart, what anger we feel, or how frightened or thankful we are, we again miss the opportunity for a blessing! However, if we make an effort to honestly share our thoughts and concerns with our Heavenly Father and have the faith to believe that He understands our fears, He will help allay them, bring peace to our heart, teach us, and bring us yet another blessing in the process. Communication is usually described as an exchange of words, but we also communicate in other ways, some conscious and some of which we are unaware. We may send a thought to our Heavenly Father, wear a facial expression which others can read, type in a set of consonants viewed from a cell phone, fold our arms, lean away from someone, or even use sign language as a way to communicate.

Communication also occurs when we talk to *ourselves.* When we feel fear or joy, when we are hungry or cold, when we consciously stop ourselves from saying something hurtful, when we feel the need to flee a dangerous situation, and when we search our heart for those thoughts and behaviors which may be displeasing to God, we are communicating with ourselves. This very necessary personal communication is termed "introspection", is often inspired by the Holy Spirit and is yet another blessing we have received from God. Sadly, it is one which we rarely credit Him for, even though this type of self examination can make a huge difference in our spiritual development.

It is very important to recognize that a blessing from God is not a gift. A gift is something which, once given, we can keep, while *a blessing is something we can lose.* Scripture makes this clear. For example, in the book of Job we learn that God blessed Job with many possessions, yet allowed them all to be taken away, and we can also read that Abraham was asked to sacrifice the son with which he was blessed and through their hardships their faith was brought to light. Thus, when we pray, we should ask God to *help* us recognize and appreciate His blessings and to help us understand how He communicates with us!

When we seek to build our relationship with God we do our best to talk with Him as we would with someone we dearly love. He recognizes our effort and our need, and provides what is best for us. But when we lack the desire, and do not develop the ability to closely communicate with God, our concerns can overpower us and cause depression and a hopelessness which saps our strength. Furthermore, words which attempt to describe our emotions are often inadequate, thus can defy proper expression. While God knows everything we feel, often those around us do not.

Interestingly, a "good bedside manner" is the term we use when our caregivers communicate well and is a quality we appreciate. Yet we often neglect our own "bedside manner" when in conversation with others, with God, and even with ourselves! When every communication is offered with honesty and an open heart, it contributes to a better understanding of one another. It helps us learn what values we hold and what hopes we have and can thereby build trust. We develop trust when those with whom we converse respond with a true interest in our well being and offer us their heartfelt warmth. When we sense a sincere desire to connect, and an understanding of our message, we are pleased by that conversation. However, we rarely ask ourselves whether or not our own words contribute to a conversation which is satisfying and beneficial, nor examine how our words may be received by others. Therefore, we should be careful to examine our personal communication skills in this light and consider that when we come away from a conversation feeling let down, it may be because *we* have not offered an effective level of communication or that our conversation is too selfish to support a more satisfying exchange.

God blesses an examination of our conversation in this light because He knows that we can learn from it. He understands that words can help *or* hurt and that many of us have to work harder to develop a level of exchange which benefits everyone and becomes an encouraging force rather than a neutral or negative one. Choosing our words carefully and learning how to express *love* through our words is a precious skill which helps us overcome many circumstances. While we are influenced by the conversation of others, we too influence through our conversations and God willingly helps us in this endeavor. In fact, one of the blessings of communicating well with our Heavenly Father is that it automatically helps us communicate well with others.

When we do communicate well and view our circumstances with our spiritual eyes rather than the negativity sometimes offered by our physical circumstances we can become an inspiration to others. This has the beneficial effect of lifting our own spirits as well. It is vital that we understand that an *inadequate* conversation can limit the growth of trust. Becoming a willing and *working* partner to a *godly* interaction can allay fear, heal disagreements, and allow the heart and mind to relax. Judgment inhibits trust while love enhances trust through an honest interest in one's family, aspirations, concerns, talents and hobbies, and willingly shares their own.

Prayer and faith add a godly dimension to our exchanges and brings us the blessing that *whatever* the circumstances, our Heavenly Father is in our corner and looks after us….therefore nothing can happen without His okay! This gives us courage even when we face dire circumstances. If we open our heart to *the blessing* of the learning process which God provides within all circumstance, we allow it to make of us a better person. We gain more empathy for others, more appreciation for those who help us, and a greater willingness to accept God's will for our lives.

Since God often shines through our weakness, and through that weakness teaches us to recognize His hand in our life, our faith is strengthened even when we cannot immediately see those results. God can turn our circumstance into a blessing even when the outcome is *not* what we'd hoped. His blessing helps us find happiness *despite* our circumstances and is the state in which God wants us to live. God does *not* look upon our failures; He looks into our hearts. He looks for our *striving* and our *desire* to do what is right, and for our *desire* to learn, and to trust Him. He sees all things...especially those things which we try to hide from others.... sometimes even from our selves. He understands why we feel as we do and wants to teach us how to find peace and joy *regardless of our circumstances.*

God helps us so we can learn how much He loves us. It is through His love that we learn how to truly love others. The love which mankind knows can be fickle and conditional, while the love God provides is stedfast, endless, and unconditional. Satan, on the other hand, promotes hate and wants us to be angry with God and to blame Him rather than trust Him. He does not want us to recognize God's blessings. Satan wants to break our faith so that he can prolong his life by preventing God from finding faithful souls for His new kingdom.

Some scoff at matters pertaining to faith or religion and view scripture with a closed mind and heart. Yet God wants *all* men saved and has made equal provision for everyone who ever lived or died to do so. But in the process, God also wants all men to experience peace and happiness *despite* the circumstances through which they might live, and so He blesses us. Looking for His blessings helps us "know" God. And honest self-communication and deep introspection will help us recognize the shortcomings which keep us from the fullness of His blessings. Therefore as we listen to ourselves and open our heart to God and to the marvel of the blessings He provides, we need never be afraid and can rest assured that we are working toward that day when the Lord returns.

Without introspection and self-communication we can easily fall into complacency. Complacency supports the belief that we need no further correction, no further improvement, nor do we need to learn of God and follow

His statutes. We might forget that the Bride God seeks for His Son is to be perfect, and is to work toward that perfection right up until the return of Christ.

The story you are about to read is about the importance of recognizing God's blessing even when we face terrible circumstances. It is a story about how our troubles help us recognize the true attitudes which live in our heart and soul and about the guilt we feel when we suddenly realize that we do not want to accept our circumstances as something God allows because it can serve a purpose in our lives.

The goal of this book is to demonstrate how and why we fall prey to our fears and how they are often related to loss. It is to explain in story-form the spiritual side of our deep desire to retain our physical and material possessions when faced with the possibility of losing them. It is about how we often have no idea that we have been clinging in pride to what we believe we own and, like the rich man who was asked to leave his riches to follow Christ, we too may find it difficult to give these things up. This story is about Caleb and the many challenges he faces. Those of you who have read my novels will remember that Caleb is Sarah's older brother and comes from a background of faith. He is someone we might expect would always be strong in faith;

never shaken. He is a man of integrity; a man of strength and goodness, but one who is also human and thus can succumb to his worries and fears. His struggle demonstrates how devastating a health issue can be, how Satan uses it to increase fear and decrease faith. Caleb's challenges demonstrate how God works through dire circumstances to teach us; to create the awareness that all we are and all we have has been provided by Him and are blessings, *not gifts.*

As the story unfolds Caleb begins to understand that a gift, once given, is something we can keep, while a blessing is something which we can lose. It is a harsh lesson, but one which was necessary to Caleb and his wife Ann; one which helps them see where they need to make a change in their life to help them become worthy. And it is through their honest communication and introspection that Ann and Caleb finally learn where they have fallen short. They also realize that if they had not experienced their difficult circumstances they may never have recognized their shortcomings and, like the five foolish virgins, may not have been ready for the coming of the Lord. This story is also about the power of Satan and why he attacks the children of God. It is about the spiritual warfare which exists between God and Satan and why that war is all about us. It is about how we must learn to recognize, resist, and overcome those attacks to become the person God wants us to become. It is about the importance of introspection when we are attacked and when we enter difficult circumstances and....as we commune with God.

I hope that you enjoy this story, and along with Ann and Caleb, learn that God loves us so much that he blesses us in many ways and that through our trials and tribulations He patiently and gently teaches us how to become all that we can become. I hope that you will be inspired by this story which began with the development of a wonderful faith in Grandma, the heroin in my first novel, whose struggles inspired her to hand down a legacy of faith to her grandchildren and many future generations. While my novels are a continuing saga, each can be read separately, each tell a different story, each deals with a different human tragedy, each describes God's incredible love for us, and each shows how scripture covers our every need. May God bless you and keep you always and may He touch your heart with the desire to learn of Him.

Helen Glowacki

"And the Spirit, and the bride say,

Come.

And let him that heareth say,

Come,

and let him that is athirst come.

And whosoever will,

let him take the water of life freely."

Revelation 22:17

TABLE OF CONTENTS

****

Excerpt from:

The Lord hath appeared

of old unto me,

saying Yea,

I have loved thee with

an everlasting love:

therefore with lovingkindness

have I drawn thee.

Jeremiah 31:3

Chapter One

A NIGHT TO REMEMBER

Ann stood at the French style sliding glass doors in the family room and looked out onto the long lawn which was edged with beautifully manicured shrubs. It was raining so hard that she could hardly see the new spring flowers she'd recently planted. Even the garden lights were affected by the rain and barely illuminated the path which wound its way around the plantings. All the natural light which would normally come from the setting sun had disappeared even though it was only just past 7 pm.

Caleb was late again. He'd phoned to tell her that he had just been informed that three of the many pallets of roofing materials delivered just a short while ago were not a match to the other materials. Since the driver of the truck was not too far down the road and could easily return to correct the error, Caleb had phoned him asking if he wanted to make the exchange right away. Since this would save the driver the extensive paperwork which a delivery error, alternate pick-up and new delivery date would entail, the driver was happy to return. This would require Caleb to remain at work until the exchange was completed.

Ann was very proud of Caleb. He was dedicated to his work and to his workers and was known for his hard work and admirable integrity. He was a man who was always thinking of others and always doing his best to make the workload of others both enjoyable and efficiently accomplished. He was highly respected by his co-workers because they recognized his sincere concern for their welfare. He never asked anyone to do something which he would not pitch in and do right next to them if necessary. Ann knew that his men loved him and worked hard to meet the goals he set for their projects. He gave his home and family, his friends and church work the same degree of effort and with the same happy attitude.

Caleb was currently working on the construction of a huge indoor shopping mall. It was the largest job he'd ever tackled and was providing him with an incredible range of responsibilities. He was learning something new every day and would come home excited and filled with awe about the challenges he had encountered and what they had been able to accomplish. Ann often had to hide the smile which crept onto her face as she witnessed his enthusiasm. His joy made her joyful. Yet taking the mall job in the first place wasn't an easy decision for him and it certainly wasn't made without much research, much thought, and many prayers. The "What if's" had raged through his mind, and no matter how hard he tried to stifle his concerns, he could not stop thinking about all the parts which needed to come together to make his acceptance of the job work for them. For a while it seemed that the job offer was all they ever talked about.

Ann too had worried about the job offer, wondering how such a huge project could be successfully navigated... especially on top of Caleb's other responsibilities. He loved to spend time with the family, he ran his own construction business, he was active in church, and now he was considering adding the huge mall undertaking to everything else. But Ann also knew Caleb and understood that this challenge was not only a career boost, but also would be very stimulating and educational for him....and beneficial to their future. Ann knew that Caleb could do anything he set his mind to....with God's help!

The mall was to be anchored in each of its five corners by a large department store. Each of these stores were to be attached to one another by a series of smaller retail stores which would form a ring around a center lobby and contain a food court above and to the back of that lobby. The ceilings were so high that rather than the two story structure it appeared to be, it was built to accommodate the height of a four or five story structure.

Caleb had been given a set of the drawings to bring home as he pondered whether or not he would take the job. He pored over the initial blueprints and became more excited with each discovery! He'd call Ann to come and look at what he'd discovered on the plans, and would excitedly explain what the drawings meant. From the exposed steel beams to the spiral stairs and elegant escalators, to the interior roof fascades of the boutiques and more elegant restaurants, he was enthralled to think that he would be instrumental in their creation. Ann could not help but think: *What an incredible opportunity this will be for him!* But then she'd think: *Will he be taking on too much?*

But, as the decision making moment loomed closer, Caleb constantly pondered the pros and cons and sometimes asked Ann why he even thought that could take on such a huge endeavor....and with people he hardly knew. He'd wonder why they had chosen him for this project rather than a larger firm, but then speak about the opportunity he was being offered, the learning experience he would garner, and the name recognition it would give his business.

At the end of all their discussions, he and Ann would pray and ask God to direct their path and bring about only what He wanted for him....for them....for their family. He'd tell God about the research he'd done, about how he'd talked further with Ann, about how he had brought his dilemma to his minister, and that he had even tithed something extra so he would make the right decision and have the blessing they would surely need for such a massive undertaking.

From a practical point of view, he'd think about the other people connected to this huge project. He'd met many of the partners in the huge firm which specialized in building and managing malls all over the country and similar to the one he'd be working on. He liked them. Ann had met them too, and both had remarked that they seemed down to earth, no-nonsense, fact seeking men who were trying to build an organization of importance and one of service to the community. They also seemed to be men of integrity.... and of faith... which was what finally convinced Caleb to take the job and Ann to agree.

As Ann stood now at the window, watching the lightning illuminate the wind-driven rain, she remembered that it had been almost two years ago since Caleb had learned that a mall was to be built at the outskirts of town. *How could two years have already gone by* she wondered? *Was it really that long ago?*

Caleb had been approached by one of the attorneys for the huge international corporation which specialized in the construction and management of large indoor shopping malls. The attorney explained that the corporation consisted of a bevy of investors and employed lawyers and accountants and architects who would lay the groundwork for their activities. They were looking for someone local to be on their team, someone who understood the town, understood the people, and their hopes and dreams, wishes and concerns for their lives and for the growth of the area.

They had also assured Caleb that the company's accountants had carefully estimated what their costs would be, what profits to expect, and how long the process from blueprints to approvals to the grand opening would take. The lawyers would draw up the myriad of contracts they would require and address any legal matters that arose. The architects would provide blueprints for zoning approvals and construction inspections. Caleb had been both impressed and intimidated.

As a custom builder and architect himself with a stellar reputation for excellent work, Caleb had a flourishing business which had allowed him to create a savings account and to pay off the mortgage on the house he'd built for his family. He had been content until the economic downturn had hit, business had slowed, and regulations appeared which were totally unreasonable and foolishly costly.

Everything he'd ever built had been constructed with very high standards and far above the required code but these new regulations, which had been recently issued, seemed to have little to do with code and much to do about fees and fines and paperwork, and addressed some very foolish and usually redundant requirements.

In fact, Caleb had been overwhelmed by the number of new regulations and by the time and effort they took to read and understand. He lamented the amount of documentation these regulations demanded and became frustrated by how long it took him to complete. He was relieved when Ann had stepped in to help sort them out and keep him on top of what was required. He'd been so grateful for her help and her easy explanation of complicated issues and Ann had basked in her new found ability to help him.

With the advent of the economic downturn, their business had moved toward renovation rather than the new construction Caleb loved, but it still provided a sufficient income for what the family required, and they were thankful for God's grace in providing for them.

When this new job offer came along, they discussed the pros and cons of Caleb turning the new business his own company received over to the crew he employed and devoting all his time to the mall. Because of the large scope of the mall project, they also discussed the fact that accepting this job would surely take time away from the family. Yet it was an excellent opportunity for him to learn and grow. In the end, and after much prayer and a multitude of discussion, they decided to accept the offer. Caleb became the local liaison for the huge new mall and he would be responsible for overseeing the work and keeping the project on track.

A huge and very close thunder strike brought Ann from her thoughts of the past to her worry about why Caleb was so late. She wondered if Caleb was still at the construction site or was already on his way home. The rain was coming down in buckets and the thunder and lightning grew so formidable that though the covered patio outside the door at which she stood separated her from the weather, she pulled away from the door fearing how close the lightning strikes seemed to be.

Ann walked into the main area of the house and checked on the dinner she'd saved for Caleb's arrival. Andrew and Lorraine were playing one of the spelling games they received for Christmas and were oblivious to the weather. Andrew, born in August of 2006 was almost six years old and Lorraine, born in November of 2008 was a little more than three and one half years old. They both loved to play "school" and shared the responsibility of being "teacher". It was amazing that Lorraine always seemed to give Andrew a run for his money in terms of spelling abilities even though she was so young!

The children were sprawled out on their tummies in front of the huge stone-front fireplace which spanned one entire wall of the two-storied family room. They had placed the spelling game in front of them and when one of them made a spelling error, the other would roll with laughter turning from tummy to back on the deep pile of the Oriental carpet covering the dark stained hardwood floors. Ann smiled with joy as she watched the children. She thanked God for the great blessing the children were. She also recognized and was so thankful for the blessing they each had in Caleb who loved God with all his heart and taught his family by the example of his own loving words and actions. Caleb was a wonderful role model to their entire family and Ann felt so blessed that she and the children had been given such a special husband and father.

She and Caleb had designed and built their home themselves and specifically built and designed it to accommodate family fellowships. They'd taken great care to plan the kitchen to be open to the huge family room and large dining area so those who might be cooking could still join in the conversations in those rooms. One wall of the family room was made up of darkly stained French style glass doors which looked out and through the roofed patio and over the garden. The unique feature of the doors was how they opened and folded out of sight to allow the inside and outside areas to blend. The cathedral ceilings of the kitchen, family room and dining area created an airy feeling while complimenting the massive stone wall of the fireplace. The dark stained beams across the high ceilings matched the color of the hardwood floors below. The room could seat a large number of people because of the huge stone ledge in front of the fireplace which spanned an entire wall. The ledge had been fitted with cushions which matched the covering of the dining room chairs, the trim on the valances above the doors and windows, and also two of the easy chairs in the family room. Thus the entire space was color coordinated in fabric as well as in wood tone.

The family gatherings were great fun. Everyone loved to play games, many of which were bible quizzes and charades. Some games were very silly but so much fun that they all laughed together....and all enjoyed them because both children and adults could join in. The various seating areas allowed everyone to gather close to one another in one huge group, and for the children to join in as well. However, the room also provided many little areas in which some of the children could play another game. The families cherished their time together and took turns hosting a fellowship every month. They cooked together, and joked about many of the role reversals they found in the group as one of the men would ice a cake and one of the women would carve the roast.

They shared their triumphs and their heartaches. They prayed for one another and they rejoiced in their faith. They were dedicated to being a good friend and role model to one another and to their children. They opened their heart and their homes to everyone in their church and to anyone else they met who touched their heart or seemed in need. Through these efforts their family circle grew, their friendships deepened, and their faith became rock solid.

Ann remembered that one of their most poignant experiences of faith had occurred when their daughter Lorraine had been born and they learned that she had a heart defect which would have to be corrected surgically. She had been hospitalized to repair the defect in February, 2009 when she was only two months old. It had been touch and go for a while, but finally Lorraine pulled through and they all thanked God for His loving care.

However, later that year, in late September, Lorraine was again hospitalized. She had developed a fever and the physicians were concerned that this could damage her heart. Sitting in the hospital waiting room, Caleb remembered the notice he'd received from their family attorney informing him that well before Grandma died, she'd composed a letter for each family member. The lawyer explained that Grandma had instructed him to hold the letters until such time that a family emergency occurred. Thus the attorney had given Caleb the letters when he learned that Lorraine would need heart surgery. But because the attorney told Caleb that Grandma's instructions were that he was not to distribute the letters unless there was an emergency, and with Lorraine *already* on the mend, Caleb decided to keep the letters in his safe until he somehow *knew* that it was time to give them out.

However, with Lorraine's life in danger that September, Caleb decided that it was time for him to claim his letter. He knew that once he'd read it, he'd know whether or not to give the other letters to his brother and sister. Thus Caleb made the split second decision to leave the hospital, get his letter and share its contents with Ann. Something in his heart told him that he and Ann needed to read Grandma's letter right away. Caleb left the waiting room but was back at the hospital in record time. When Ann and Caleb read the letter together while waiting for the doctor to talk to them about Lorraine, the miracle they saw in Grandma's words helped them to know, beyond a shadow of a doubt, that Lorraine would be okay and that God was with them, comforting them, letting them know how carefully He looked after them. That night, sitting in the cold drab waiting room reading the letter which Grandma had written long before her death and had so meticulously arranged that it arrive so many years later, made their faith and awe of God's love for them soar! They later learned that in the other letters too, what Grandma had written proved to be a personal miracle of faith for all of them. Grandma had chosen one or more Bible verses for each couple to read. She explained that these were to strengthen them for what they were experiencing at the time they would read the letters. She had written them three and one half years earlier, before she had died, and had placed them in the care of her attorney with instructions to give Caleb the letters whenever the family was experiencing a difficult time. Thus when the attorney heard about Lorraine's impending surgery, he decided that this was the "difficult time" to which Grandma had been referring. Caleb however, at that time, had decided to hold the letters because Lorraine was already on the mend. But now.... with a second worry for Lorraine's well being, Caleb somehow sensed that it was time to open the letters.

Caleb read the letter addressed to him and Ann aloud, and both were amazed that in Grandma's elegant writing, written so long ago, was a verse from Exodus 33:22 whose words were suddenly a miracle. They read: *"I will put thee in a clift of the rock, and will cover thee with my hand."* He had read the letter aloud and but then handed Ann the letter so she could see it for herself. They looked at one another in awe and together exclaimed: "This is amazing. God has spoken to us and comforted us! Lorraine will be okay!" The miracle they recognized was that the name of the hospital in which they sat and in which Lorraine lay fighting for her life was Rockclift General Hospital and the hospital had not been built, nor had a name been chosen for it until well after Grandma had died! Further, how would she have known that any of them would be in any dire straits? Thus, the verse she provided in her letter and just for them was surely divinely inspired! From that moment on they knew that Lorraine would be okay and that God, through what Grandma had written so many years ago, was telling them that He loved them and was still looking after them! It was experiences such as these which made their faith so strong… and as Grandma had taught them….it was allowing those experiences to live in one's heart *as fact* and not as coincidence which touched God's heart. *"Look for the blessing"* Grandma would say, *"and you will find it."*

Later, when giving out the letters which Grandma had written for the others, and sharing what she had written to them, they all emerged with tears of amazement and gratitude. Caleb had invited the family to his home to give them their letters, explain the circumstances by which he'd received them, and explain the instructions about when they should be opened. Each decided to read their letters right away and shared with one another the troubles which they were currently facing. When each read their letter and saw how Grandma's words perfectly fit their current circumstances, they all realized that God had worked this miracle through Grandma to strengthen their faith.

As Ann recalled that experience, she felt better and less worried about Caleb out so late and in such a thundering rain. But just as she seemed to put her fears aside, another loud burst of thunder struck and a bright flash of lightning appeared in the backyard. She both saw and heard the sound of a huge branch breaking off one of the trees in the yard and then she heard the branch hit the ground. She was relieved that the tree had been too far away to hit the house. She worried then anew, knowing that while God always looked after them, there were no guarantees that they would not have their faith tested by going through some very difficult times. Life was hard, life was a testing ground where the children of God would face many trials and tribulations as they set their face toward Heaven and an eternal future with God. Satan wanted to break their faith to prevent God from obtaining the number of faithful souls He wanted for His new kingdom.

Ann gathered the children to her side and asked them if they wanted to pray together. "Daddy needs the angel protection just like we do, so let's ask God to surround him and his truck with angels as he makes his way home!" They bowed their heads and kneeled around the large ottoman near the fireplace and each prayed that God would look after Caleb and would send His angels to protect and surround him. They thanked their Heavenly Father for His love and stedfastness despite their faults and failings, and asked Him to help them be overcomers and worthy to go with Christ when He returned for His Bride. They ended their prayer with the plea that God would send His Son soon for the First Resurrection where the faithful would finally be once again with Christ. Ann helped the children put their game away and get ready for bed. As usual they displayed an amazing burst of energy just before bedtime and gleefully, after their bath and once in their pajama's, they jumped on Lorraine's bed and then did a somersault before finally settling down for their evening prayer. They prayed at the side of Lorraine's bed and when each completed their prayer, Andrew and Ann tucked Lorraine into her comforter and kissed her before turning toward Andrew's room next door. Ann tucked Andrew into his bed, kissed him, and walked back to the family room.

Looking into the yard through the back doors once again, Ann saw that the rain was still pounding the ground, but the thunder and lightning seemed to have moved further away. She could still see flashes of light in the sky, but heard no further thunder. She walked back to the fireplace, sat in the leather chair and tried to read, but her mind kept wandering to what could be keeping Caleb so late and to her worries about the bad weather. *Why hadn't he called again when he realized that he would be later than he'd thought when he'd first told her he'd be late?* "Keep him safe Lord, she said quietly. *"Please keep him safe"*.

Chapter Two

WHEN EVERYTHING GOES WRONG

As Caleb drove to work that morning, he'd been exhilarated by the beautiful weather. The air was crisp and dry, the sun warm and bright, and the sky an incredible blue with large puffy white clouds moving lazily across its surface. The men loved this kind of weather and often accomplished more than expected when they were presented with conditions such as these. There were many days when the men had to work in less than desirable conditions; the worst being high winds and a driving rain.

Thus, as he pulled onto the acres of construction he knew that the men would be smiling in anticipation of a good day while they sipped their morning coffee.

Caleb was expecting a delivery of the roofing materials which were scheduled to be hoisted right from the truck to the roof. He wanted the materials placed safely and correctly on the roof and wanted the delivery to be complete, rather than require a second delivery. It was such a hassle when what was ordered was not what was delivered... or a partial delivery was made. *A lot of extra time and effort and...paperwork,* he thought. He decided to forestall any problems by asking his roofing foreman to check the pallets carefully before signing off on the order.

As he approached the men circling around the coffee wagon, most already holding steaming cups of coffee, he could sense their interest in what Keith was telling them. Keith was affectionately known as "Preacher". In fact many of the men had acquired nicknames from their co-workers... usually because of a particular habit or interest they had expressed. Preacher was talking about the "Our Family" church magazine he'd just read and specifically about one of the articles which had caught his attention. He aimed his remarks at Joe who was always disputing

Preacher's remarks. "Hey Joe, didja know that scripture teaches us that there is an ongoing war between God and Satan and that we are what the battle is all about. Satan is alive and well and operates in our lives to break our faith by breaking our bodies and our spirit. He can also attack our self-worth to break our faith, or create an indifferent attitude to prevent us from having faith. He works best when we are not aware of what he does. He does not want us to learn what God teaches us through scripture and wants us to live and die in a state of unawareness. He does not want us to know that our fears and worries, anxieties and hopelessness place us under his captivity and takes away our desire to be close to God and even worse, robs us of our ability to trust God."

"Come on Preacher," Joe replied, "You don't really believe that there is an evil *elf* out there running around in a red suit who is trying to hurt us, do you? I mean...get real!" And Joe began to prance around holding a pitch fork, laughing, and pretending to give everyone the evil eye.

"Yeah, I do", Preacher replied. "And you should too! Evil is very dangerous Joe, and no one is immune, not even you, so you should be careful about what you say and do."

"Ahh well"' Joe quipped as he flexed the muscles in his arm, "I'm a pretty tough guy and could probably take him on! 'Hey there evil one in the red suit, wanna arm wrestle?'"

The men laughed nervously as, believer or not, they were hesitant to play games with anything that could potentially be so dangerous.

"Be careful what you call down onto yourself, o ye of little faith", Preacher quipped. But under his good natured demeanor, as he began to walk toward his work area he felt disappointed that the other men, some of whom he knew were believers, had not backed him up.

What Preacher didn't realize was that some of the men had felt a strong sense of unease as they wondered if Preacher was right in warning Joe to be careful about challenging Satan. Others simply laughed. And because the conversation had become uncomfortable, they broke into smaller groups, and began moving toward their work area.

Caleb would have backed up what Preacher had said, but he'd arrived as the conversation was winding down and hadn't fully understood the challenge. As the group broke up, Caleb ordered his own coffee and carried the cup to the trailer which housed his office. He wanted to focus on the events which he knew he had to tackle that day.

Despite wanting to direct his thoughts to his work list, his mind kept going back to what Preacher had said about the danger of Joe challenging Satan. Caleb knew that Satan was dangerous and far stronger than man. But he also knew that God was stronger than Satan and with God's protection, even the heartache which Satan was allowed to bring to mankind could be turned into a blessing.

Accosted with a myriad of questions as he stepped into the trailer and thus became available to his men, he forgot his worry and began to formulate the work schedule. He informed his men that the roofing materials were expected to be delivered that day and explained that they would be transferred directly from the truck to the roof. He opened the blueprints of the buildings to show them where he wanted the truck and where he wanted the materials placed.

"The large cache of granite rocks which we are using for the foundation fascia, were delivered yesterday. We had them dumped close to the foundation over here on the north side. We still have an issue with mud in this area, so let's direct the truck to the south side where the landscape slopes away from the building and can carry off any rain we might get. This will allow the truck the best access to where we need the pallets placed. Everyone okay with this? Any questions? Problems?"

As the men turned to leave, Caleb added the words: "Each of you are ultimately responsible for your men and must always evaluate the danger, the work load, and the nuances of what is occurring around you so we can all stay safe." And then he wondered why he'd said that and whether or not Preacher's words were some sort of an omen.

Come on now Caleb, he said to himself, *why so morose....get with it...it's a beautiful day! God knows how formidable Satan is and as long as we strive to overcome and do our best, He will help us.*

While the day had started out with perfect weather, late in the afternoon the clouds began to roll in and the winds kicked up and finally the rain came. Caleb worried about the delivery of the roofing materials, about how the mud might impede the truck and about how the rain might affect their visibility. He also worried about how safe it was for the truck's crane to lift the pallets from the truck to the roof over four stories up while it was raining… and possibly when there were high winds. *The driver will know*, Caleb told himself, *He will not risk an accident.*

Soon thereafter the truck arrived and despite the rain and the wind, the transfer went well. As the driver lifted his materials to the roof, every pallet was carefully stabilized against the wind and rain by Caleb's men. Once the pallets were in place and the foreman had signed off for the number of pallets ordered and received, the driver began to pull out of the construction site, moving slowly to avoid the mud at the side of the road. Caleb watched as the driver turned the corner and disappeared from sight, sighing with relief that the weather hadn't seemed to matter. In a few days, the pallets would begin to disappear as the roofers used the materials and the roof was completed. All they needed was a couple of days of dry weather!

Suddenly Joe came running up to Caleb, breathless from his sprint. "Caleb, there are three pallets which do not match the other materials. Either our materials are still on the truck… and these belong to another job…. or someone made a mistake when they loaded the truck."

Caleb considered this information for a moment and then said, "Thanks for catching this Joe. If I phone the driver, and he does have the correct materials on the truck, and he wants to correct the error, we can save him another trip out here..... and we can save him all the paperwork necessary to fixing this error. I hope that I can reach him"

Caleb called the driver who pulled to the side of the road and checked his bill of lading. He knew that he had another delivery to make that day of similar sized pallets....and may have removed pallets belonging to that second order rather than taking those belonging to Caleb's order. This meant that he'd have two angry customers....and an angry boss if the error wasn't corrected right away. He decided to return and correct the error now rather than face admitting to the mistake later on.

"Thanks Caleb for catching this...I would have had to take a lot of guff for this mistake and would have to make another trip out here.....and perhaps bear the anger of the other customer who would not be getting their correct order."

Caleb and Joe hurried to the roof to identify the incorrect pallets before the driver returned. Preacher followed them to the roof hoping that with more help they could get the exchange done more quickly. They would have to determine whether or not the pallets which would have to be exchanged were wedged in with other pallets. That could make the exchange more difficult.

As soon as they reached the roof, each of the men walked over to the safety harnesses knowing that it was company policy to wear the harness when on the roof. The heavy leather of the harness and the rope attachments were cumbersome and weighed the men down, but each understood that it was to keep them safe and thus worth the inconvenience. The three men slipped the harness over their shoulders and fastened the leg straps to secure the harness to their bodies. Joe and Preacher took turns hooking one another's harness to the long ropes which were attached to the center of the roof which, if they fell, would keep them from falling off the edge.

Then they turned to check the pallets, and sure enough, three of the correct pallets would have to be removed in order to retrieve and then replace the incorrect pallets. Caleb phoned the driver again to let him know what had to be done.

As Caleb marked the three incorrect pallets, worrying about the fading light, he noticed that although the rain had stopped, the surface was still slippery. He warned Joe and Preacher of the danger since they were the two men who would be on the roof to hook the pallets to the crane for removal, to guide the crane to placing the correct pallets in the correct location, and to be sure that the remaining pallets were well secured.

Caleb decided that though both Preacher and Joe could handle the job, he too would remain on the roof to help in case they needed another hand. Caleb carefully described what they needed to do since they would have to move some of the correct pallets to get at the ones which would have to be taken off the roof. The men grunted their understanding and approval. Caleb asked them to hook up a few temporary lights in case the job took longer than he thought it would and the natural light was lost before they finished the job. As the truck pulled back onto the construction site, Caleb phoned Ann to let her know that he would be late.

The three men sat on one of the pallets as they watched the truck slowly back in toward the south side of the building. They knew that it would take time for the driver to get everything ready. He had to identify the pallets which would come off the truck and make room for those he would bring back down to the truck. As the driver worked, Preacher, Joe and Caleb began to talk while perched high above the ground on a pallet of material. As they watched the driver set up the crane more than four stories below them. Preacher re-opened his earlier conversation with Joe.

"Joe, you are making a big mistake not to acknowledge that there is a Satan and that he has 1/3 of all the original angels from heaven helping him cause havoc here on earth. It is only our acknowledgement and recognition of what is occurring through Satan which can help us battle against those spirits before they become entrenched and become more difficult to fight. Learning who and what is *really* to blame for our circumstances is important so we can be armed to protect ourselves."

"Come on Preacher, if that's true then why doesn't everyone worry and cower, and know all this? How are we supposed to "arm" ourselves? And why would Satan do this anyway? And why would God allow it?"

"You should know this stuff….and *would* if you ever read the Bible!" Preacher replied.

"Now, now, let's not argue here", Caleb interjected. "But let me say Joe that I agree with Preacher. The reason Satan brings harm to us is to break the faith of God's children. When God finds the number of faithful souls He wants for His new kingdom of peace, Satan will be bound forever. All evil will be bound. And Satan wants to avoid that…. at all costs. That's why he attacks us."

"Yeah'" Preacher added, "In fact, Matthew 8:16 explains that there were many who were overcome by Satan in Christ's time and when Christ cast these spirits out, the people were healed. *"When the evening was come, they brought unto him many that were possessed with devils: and he cast out the spirits with his word, and healed all that were sick."* The keywords here are "healed" and "cast out" and explains that the ungodly spirit kept the man bound by something he could not escape. Those satanic spirits can also make us believe that what we fear and experience can *never* be overcome and that we will never be happy again. But when we replace those thoughts with the promises God provides for us, we begin to remember those positive words instead and…. when we begin to use them automatically…. we begin to trust in them. From that trust, God works His miracles and **we begin to heal because we are no longer "feeding" that spirit."**

"So what has that got to do with me?" Joe asked.

"You're captive to unbelief. And Satan uses our failures to *keep* us captive. Although, failure does not mean defeat; it means that we need to fight... again. **Each time we fight we, in essence, "practice" how to become stronger.** Every time we consciously *strive* to overcome something, we weaken that spirit. In time, any spirit seeking to keep us from trusting and following God can be broken and forced to leave. We cannot break this spirit in one single effort and may fall back and fail many times before we finally do overcome. As we said before, Satan is stronger than we are. But God is far stronger than Satan. You, my man are captive to the spirit of unbelief *and* complacency," Preacher added with a grin.

"Ya know Preacher my friend, I appreciate your faith and that you know so much about it, but for me, well, I'm a simple man and I don't go to church very often, I don't read the Bible, and I don't think about those things. But believe me, I like that *you* do....however, I don't appreciate your putting *me* down! If I ever want to know more, I will know where to go, but I am fine with my life as it is!"

"Ahh Joe, you're lucky that all is well in your life and therefore you don't 'need' God, but someday you will...someday you will ask for His help."

"Okay Preacher, here's the real deal....I do have a concern...let's see how you suggest I fix it. My daughter had a very bad marriage and is finally out of it but in a deep depression. How can any of this religion stuff help her?"

"Ahhh.....well it can in many ways!" Caleb chimed in, "Our initial inability to rise above our debilitating emotions is an act of Satan's. We need to be loved, and nurtured through the process of change, and taught that being happy is what God wants for His children while Satan wants us to be unhappy and blame God for it. Being sad not only affects how we feel, but also affects the lives of those around us. God teaches us to love and never harm others, and His words always tell us the truth and always work to bring us into freedom. Freedom under God brings us joy and peace. When we truly believe that God is more powerful than any circumstance; that God loves us and promises to bring us through our difficult circumstances, we will not remain captive to Satan. In fact, often that very circumstance which we have lived through becomes an incredible blessing for us while teaching us empathy for others who suffer similar circumstances. We may be being groomed to become a blessing for others because we did overcome... and now have developed the love and compassion to help others when they go through similar circumstances. Joe....God has probably already lined up a wonderful new husband for your daughter.....and if he's a man who loves God, he'll treat your daughter well....so yeah....if she comes to church she can learn this, meet good people, and have a better chance for happiness!"

Preacher chimed in saying, "However, if we remain unaware of the power of Satan and the power of his cohorts, or how easily we can become trapped, we cannot understand free will, recognize the choices we are afforded, or the consequences of those choices. If we do not know that Satan instigates our negative thoughts, we may not say "NO" to them. We may instead allow them to implant fear in our hearts. We may never think to *flee* from them by immersing ourselves in the fellowship of believers and in God's words. We may forget to replace the negative thoughts with the positive words of God which will weaken that spirit. So....we *stay* depressed and afraid."

"Because all of us fall into despair from time to time or into troubled circumstances, God asks us to develop and practice compassion and offer it to others", Caleb added. "The world is too dangerous to our spiritual well-being for us not to be armed with God's warnings and promises and not to develop the courage to stand up and fight for the blessing He so freely provides. God's children must offer their love and their patience, instruction, and prayer to those who are trapped, and help them recognize when Satan attacks, and what they can do to fight back. Providing understanding, love, compassion, and prayer brings comfort. Providing an explanation about what God offers and the role Satan plays helps us to bypass the traps which Satan lays for us. None of us are free of these attacks though for each of us they come in a different form."

Joe nodded and seemingly in agreement added, "Well, I know that appearances can be deceiving and those who suffer usually try to hide their pain. But in time, unhappiness, and a heavy heart does reveal itself, and maybe you are right to suggest we look for ways to help even if it is simply by praying for someone we think may be carrying a heavy cross. It's true that not everyone can easily share the details of their troubles and maybe we need to tell them that we love them; that we are praying for them, and that we offer a trustworthy friendship….and then *be* trustworthy!"

"That's exactly right Joe, prayer is powerful and God always blesses us when we seek His direction. Fellowship with other believers often brings to light a story which is similar to ours; one which culminated in a wonderful blessing. This inspires those who suffer similar circumstances and gives them hope. But most importantly, when we are attacked by Satan and when we enter into a time of difficulty we must understand that we battle an enemy who is much stronger than we are, and that only with God's help will we defeat this enemy."

"Well….." Joe said, "That makes sense and maybe I *will* talk to her….you have a point. If she meets guys who are not suitable she might go through this again….but if she met a really good hearted guy, yeah…I guess you could say a 'religious' guy…..it might work the way it should."

Suddenly the walkie-talkie interrupted their conversation by blaring the notice that that the crane was on its way up to move the three pallets out of the way to make room for lifting and removing the three incorrect pallets. As the huge hook appeared, Joe grabbed it and wrestled it into position and then onto the pallet wires while talking his instructions to the driver below through the walkie-talkie.

In no time the three pallets were moved and Caleb and Preacher began to prepare for their removal. Once that was done, the first of the three new pallets was hoisted into place and then the second and these two were then properly secured. The third however would have to fit into a more specific and much tighter space. Directions flew back and forth for wedging the third and last pallet into place. Since Joe and Preacher seemed to have everything under control and Caleb did not want to appear to micro-manage, he stepped back to allow the men the room they needed to swing the final pallet into its compartment.

As Caleb placed his foot behind him, the side of his boot caught against one of the supports used to secure the pallets to the roof and he lost his balance. He fell and began to slide toward the edge of the roof. He reached out to grab the edge of the pallet support but it was too far away. He kept sliding on the rain soaked surface and then tried to grab the rope which was connected to his safety harness. Suddenly he realized that his harness had not been clipped to the security rope. As his gloved hand grasped the rope hoping to stop his slide, he felt it slip through his fingers until the clamp reached his gloved hand. His momentum was too great for his hand to hold onto the clamp. He was forced to let go because of the weight and speed of his body, and he knew then that he was in trouble. The harness was in place, but without being clamped to the safety rope, it did him no good. He tried to grab whatever he could, but it was too slippery and his momentum was too great. His body moved closer and closer to the edge.

In a last attempt to help himself, he opened his hands and used the rubberized gripping ridges in his gloves to slow his slide and to straighten his body so he could stop himself from going over the edge sideways. His body did straighten before he lost his grip, and in what seemed slow motion, he went down legs first.

Unaware of Caleb's initial loss of balance, Preacher and Joe continued to concentrate on placing the final pallet in its confined space through their ongoing instructions to the crane operator. Suddenly, hearing Caleb yell, they turned and saw Caleb disappear over the edge. Joe calmly instructed Preacher to check on Caleb and directed the driver to hold the winch and its heavy cargo in place. Then he too ran to the roofs edge to join Preacher.

Caleb was nowhere in sight but they knew that he was on the ground where none of the lamps they'd previously placed could shed their light, and where the driving rain had started once again and destroyed any hope of visibility below. Preacher ran for one of the lamps which they'd set up for their work area. Shining its light over the edge of the roof and toward the ground, they saw Caleb, sprawled... unmoving. He lay atop the pile of granite rocks which had been dumped close to the foundation on the opposite side of the structure from where the huge truck and crane had been completing its delivery.

Joe called 911 immediately and with heavy hearts both men turned back to the south side of the building where they could safely leave the roof to see to Caleb. Preacher took a minute to direct the driver to drop the last pallet in place so the truck could leave and the job could be completed. Joe went ahead hoping that he could help Caleb while they waited for the Emergency vehicle.

Preacher was back down on the ground in just a few minutes and well before the Emergency vehicle arrived. When he joined Joe he could see that Joe was holding Caleb's hand, and with tears in his eyes, was talking to him. But Caleb was not responding. However, the good news was that Caleb was still breathing. Preacher began to pray and Joe, angrier than ever before, cried out to God asking why he'd allowed this to happen.

Chapter Three

<u>REORGANIZING</u>

Caleb's phone lay on the pile of granite stones, forgotten as the paramedics dedicated their focus toward stabilizing Caleb. They knew how important it was to get him to the hospital as soon as possible but were concerned about a possible broken neck or damaged spinal cord. They worked quickly and efficiently. They inserted an IV and spoke directly with a physician at the hospital to whom they relayed Caleb's vital signs and whatever other information the doctor thought relevant. They moved him with great care after applying a neck brace and back board. Soon the ambulance was on its way to the hospital.

Now, pummeled by the rain and hidden in the dark, the lone reminder of Caleb's fall began to ring, and with no one to hear its summons, the call to his cell phone went unanswered. Ann was frantic. *Why wouldn't Caleb answer his phone?*

She'd waited to call, not wanting to interrupt him in his work, knowing he would phone her when he could. But finally, her worries overtook her self-discipline and she made the call she'd fought so hard against. It was almost nine o'clock and far past the time when Caleb should have either arrived at home or called her a second time. When Ann's call met with a message offering to carry her to his voice mail, she hung up and tried again a few minutes later with the same result. *What could have happened,* she wondered, *Could he be in an important meeting? Could he have his hands full with some job which must be completed and thus he couldn't answer the phone?*

Ann began to pace the room, wondering if she should phone Sarah. Sarah was her best friend and Caleb's sister. But as Ann thought about this option, she decided not to phone Sarah fearing that she might be worrying her for no reason. She finally decided to wait another hour. *Yes, I'll wait until ten o'clock and if Caleb has not phoned or arrived home by then.... I will phone Sarah. Perhaps then Sarah will ask her husband Matt to drive over to the job site to see if Caleb is there.*

Ann's prayer for Caleb became almost a mantra as she said over and over again, "Please God, take care of Caleb...keep him safe. Please God, take care of Caleb.... keep him safe." Her life with Caleb was steeped in their faith, and every day was a learning experience wherein if they watched for it, they could always see God's hand directing, helping, teaching, loving them. Their life revolved around their desire to be a part of God's family by learning what God asked of them and living their life according to His statutes. They marveled over the meticulous plan which God had instituted to build a people for His new kingdom, and they were in awe over the amazing information, even the laws of physics which they found in scripture. They understood how the righteousness of God and the spiritual warfare initiated by Satan created the path by which man would be required to travel in order to enter that new kingdom; one which would be free of evil and sorrow. Despite this knowledge, and despite her trust in God, fear crept into Ann's throat. She knew that sometimes life seemed unfair and that though God would bring them through their circumstances, and create a blessing from it, they would nevertheless have to endure those circumstances. She knew that Satan's goal was to break the faith of God's children. She knew how powerful Satan was and also knew that God allowed him to use that power to prove its folly. She wondered if her family would be able to endure an assault, and if so, would they would come out the other end, better people, better children of God, and have stood firm in their faith? *Would I stand firm?* She asked herself. *Everyone has their breaking point*, she thought. *But then again, God tells us that He will never give us more than we can bear.*

Ann understood that many people were faithful and loved God with all their heart....but also that many hadn't been tested therefore hadn't needed to stand firm through terrible heartache. *How do we know we can do it?* she wondered, *Oh God, why am I so worried?*

The bell rang as these questions ran through her heart and she hurried to the entry hall to answer its call. As she approached the door she could hear the heels of her shoes resound against the tiles on the floor and wondered why this made an impact on her now and she'd never even heard it before. Then, as she neared the door, she saw the revolving lights of the police car reflected through the glass of the side-panels flanking the heavy, dark stained double entry doors. She could feel her heart beating. She knew that something had happened to Caleb. She felt a wave of heat envelop her body and then such a sensation of cold that it made her suddenly shiver. There were two police officers, accompanied by an obviously devastated Joe, who stood at the front door. The lead police officer introduced himself and asked if they could come in. With no show of the raging emotions she felt inside, Ann ushered them into the family room and asked them to sit down. "Ann", Joe began, "Caleb took a bad fall and the emergency crew took him to Rockclift General Hospital.....can we bring you there? If you can't get someone to look after the children, I can stay here to do so."

Ann was surprised by how calm she sounded as she answered, "Of course. Let me phone Sarah. And Joe, if you can stay until she and Matt arrive, one of them will drive you back to the hospital." *How can I sound so calm, why am I not crying? Why am I not asking questions?* she wondered. Then she walked to the phone and made the call to Sarah, giving her a brief explanation of what had happened. Sarah said that she and Matt would be right over. Ann then left immediately with the two police officers while Joe waited for Matt and Sarah to arrive. Joe tip-toed into the two children's rooms to make sure all was well with them and to be assured that they remained undisturbed by the arrival of the police. Then he went back into the family room to wait for Matt and Sarah. Joe was still angry. As he looked around the room and saw the little plaque which quoted the words from Joshua 24:15, *"As For Me And My House, We Shall Serve The Lord"*, Joe wondered why God would have allowed this to happen to Caleb. Whenever he was here he could sense the peace in this household, which he knew emanated from the love and goodness of this family. He shook his head in disbelief and without him being aware of his actions, he clenched his fists in anger. Then his eyes rested on the well marked, well used Bible on the coffee table. In bitterness, he asked God again why He'd done this to Caleb. *How could You be a god of love if You allowed this to happen to this wonderful family...a family that loves You and follows You?*

In no time Matt and Sarah and their son Jason arrived. Jason was sound asleep and Matt carried him into the smaller guest bedroom where he tucked him into the comforter, still asleep. Matt returned to the family room and Joe gave them a quick account of what had happened. Matt told Joe that he had already alerted Josh, Caleb's younger brother about Caleb's fall and that Josh would also go to the hospital but first bring his wife Debbie here so that Sarah could accompany Josh to the hospital.

Matt and Sarah quickly bowed their head and Matt began to pray. Joe felt forced to do the same even though his anger against God and even his disbelief, made him feel like a hypocrite. The words, "Thy will be done" at the end of their prayer made Joe even more resentful. *Why* he asked himself, *why should such a cruel "will" be done or even accepted? Why would a god of love inflict harm?* But Joe said nothing…. and he and Matt left for the hospital.

Sarah had decided to send Matt to the hospital because she felt that he would be the best support for Ann at this time. He would remain strong no matter what happened. She knew that when Debbie arrived, she and her younger brother Josh would go immediately to the hospital and Matt would fill them in on the details he'd learned about Caleb.

When Matt and Joe arrived at Rockclift General, Ann was sitting in a corner of the waiting room lost in thought. She hadn't yet heard from the physicians so did not know the extent of Caleb's injuries. Joe and Matt sat next to her, but could see that Ann did not want to talk. Matt assumed that Ann was simply in continual prayer. He was partially correct. Ann did pray, but for some inexplicable reason she could not stop her thoughts from traveling to Caleb's plans for the future and how this accident might affect those plans. She tried to banish those thoughts, in fact felt guilty about them because they were about their material concerns; about what she and Caleb had wanted to do with their lives and not about what *God* might want for them or even just about Caleb's recovery.

She and Caleb had recently settled on a property they had purchased which was located on the far side of the mall. Because it was currently far from town....which would change when the mall opened and the town grew......the land was an excellent investment. Caleb had already obtained permission to build an apartment complex on the property which, when completed, would allow them to build equity and when retiring, assure them of a good income. Caleb was very excited to have this venture waiting for him when he completed the mall. To make the purchase had been a huge decision for them because it had required them to mortgage their house and cash in all their savings just for the down payment, and then to carry a second mortgage. It was a gamble, but one that Caleb had prayed over and finally decided was good for the future of their family. It left them currently in great debt. It would take at least five years before they would begin building and perhaps another three before they could realize any income from the property. Ann felt terribly guilty for thinking of these matters at a time like this. She felt that she was betraying both Caleb and God by the worries which to Ann "proved" that she was not fully trusting God. She also felt guilty for what she believed was allowing material concerns override her concern for Caleb. She didn't even know yet what his injuries were! How could she do that? She determined to force her mind back to her prayers for Caleb but then, right in the middle of a prayer, she'd suddenly find herself again thinking about their debt and how Caleb would manage. *Why am I behaving like this*, she asked herself...*Is this Satan's work?*

Against her will Ann's mind moved to how she could pick up the financial reins by getting Joe to help her run Caleb's construction business. *But what about the mall project....there is nothing that I can do there. Caleb surely couldn't be fired, but he could be required to go on disability which would not pay the bills. Could I find a job* somewhere and also run our company? Even that would not carry us. Maybe we will have to sell the new property and even our house. But, selling the house would be devastating to Caleb.....in fact to all of us.

Ann was ashamed of her thoughts. She was aware that she was allowing fear to rule. *Where is my trust in God? Why am I so sure that Caleb won't simply walk out of the hospital in a few days ready to go back to work? What is wrong with me? Why am I thinking in such negative terms? Am I in denial about Caleb's potential injuries and am transferring that to thoughts about material matters?* But Ann could not escape these thoughts as her mind raced on to reorganize their lives and to plan to do whatever was necessary for them to survive. *Reorganizing is not such a bad thing,* Ann rationalized. *God helps those who help themselves, right? I can help somehow if I just think things through!* She turned to Preacher and asked him if he thought that Caleb could lose his job with the mall. He was surprised by Ann's question. He didn't want to think about such things and something inside him told him that Ann shouldn't go there at this time either. It was too early....and maybe it would put a jinx on Caleb's recovery. "Ann, don't go there.....Caleb is going to recover. You're the one with the faith....use it...believe it!"

Matt had heard Ann's remark and Preacher's reply so he too chimed in saying "Ann, God is aware of what has happened and has a reason for it. He will look after all of you....I'm sure of that. Just keep the faith and keep on praying. When we go through heartache, God always brings us through it and brings us a blessing from it."

Ann was mortified to hear Matt's words, knowing that he was right and that she'd openly demonstrated such a terrible lack of faith. She began to cry, partly from feeling ashamed and partly because she was afraid. But then, her fears overwhelming her, she began repeating the words, "I will have to re-organize our plans; I will have to reorganize our life and try to save our home. Businesses reorganize all the time, so I should be able to accomplish this."

Matt saw immediately that Ann.... the rock in Caleb's life, the friend with quiet strength and a beautiful dedication to the family.....was terribly frightened and needed their support more than ever before. Ann had always been the one to give them the support they needed and she was now in need and the family would have to rally around her and help her through her fears. Her fear however, made Matt wonder what would happen to all of them should Caleb die and he too had to fight back such thoughts.

As quiet descended over the three, Matt wondered if burying herself in the need to reorganize their lives was a form of self preservation and a denial of the fears which were accosting Ann. *Denial is a protective mechanism, so perhaps she just needs time to adjust and once she learns more about Caleb's injuries, surely this will pass. Her concerns...and mine....and our reactions to them must just be the shock of it all,* he reasoned. "Don't worry Ann, we'll all help. We'll take care of the kids, run any errands you need taken care of, and soon Caleb will be back to his old self. God has always been there for you in the past and will be now." They prayed and asked God to help Caleb, to bless the physicians who would care for him, and to comfort Ann and remove her fear. They asked God to bind the power of Satan who wanted to plant negative thoughts in their hearts and produce the fear and anxiety which could prevent them from trusting God in this matter. Preacher picked up on what Matt said about Satan and again was reminded of his earlier discussion about evil and thought: *Maybe Joe will now see that there is such a thing as Satan, but still, why would God allow this evil to operate so freely?* To distract Ann from her fears he asked, "Matt, why wouldn't God simply put a stop to all the things Satan does....especially to someone who loves Him?"

"Well, it's more complicated than that. Our world is comprised of opposites such as hot and cold, black and white, love and hate, light and dark, good and evil, etcetera. God gave us our free will so we can choose where on this spectrum we want to be. If we choose goodness over evil and love over hate we have to do so of our own free will. Therefore God cannot interfere by *causing* us to choose one or the other. However, He does allow us to experience them all so we can learn the difference between them. Therefore God allows Satan to operate within certain parameters but only for a specific period of time. Those who choose love and goodness and spurn hate and evil recognize that perfect love and goodness comes only from God and therefore they desire to become God's children. Scripture teaches us *what* God wants us to know to help us navigate our way through a world filled with evil and learn how to protect ourselves. At some point in the near future this era of learning will end and those who chose to follow God will be invited into God's new kingdom where there will be no evil. Satan and all things evil will be bound and unable to harm mankind again. Satan, knowing that he will be stopped when God finds the number of souls He wants for His new kingdom, works diligently to break our faith and keep that number reduced."

"How do you put scripture in such a great context, Matt?"

"Well, through a combination of things. First of all, God promises to enlighten all those who seek enlightenment. He shows us His power through the might and beauty of the Creation, His orderliness through the interaction of the earth's elements, His plan through His words in scripture, His protection as we move through our daily experiences, and His love when our hearts fill with wonder and joy and wisdom as we pray. What God offers is available to all of us regardless of status or age or color or circumstance. God forgives our mistakes, loves us, and teaches us so we can become a part of something incredible in the future!"

Then Joe asked, "But why put men through this kind of stuff....you know....Caleb and all.....after all Caleb really loves God and is a believer and does what he says he'll do?"

"We are tested, Joe. Sometimes we go through terrible times, but if we stay faithful, if we trust God, He always brings us through our troubles and in the end, we always see something incredible....a blessing....emerge from what we endured....always!"

"I don't know Matt, it all seems so strange to me. But believe me I will be watching what happens here because I feel that God would have to be here for Caleb."

"Me too" Ann said defiantly.

Meanwhile, at Ann's house, and after Sarah checked on all three children and was about to sit in the family room, the doorbell rang. It was one of Ann and Caleb's neighbors and dear friend. She had seen the lights and the police car and then watched as Ann left the house with them. Her husband Richard was a physician with privileges at Rockclift Hospital. When Sarah opened the door she found Rachel there who then explained that Richard, guessing that something had happened, had phoned the hospital and learned that Caleb had been admitted. She wanted Sarah to know that Richard had gone to the hospital to see if he could help. She offered to sit with Sarah for a while as she awaited news about Caleb's condition and Sarah welcomed the company.

Hoping to keep Sarah from worrying, Rachel began a conversation about the special friendship between Caleb and her husband. "You remember Sarah....that they met when we heard from a friend that Caleb was the best builder in the area and we wanted to build a new house. We were surprised to learn that the lot on which we wanted to build was right next door to the lot Caleb had purchased for his own home....so it all seemed meant to be".

"As we got to know Ann and Caleb, we came to love and respect them and cherished our friendship. While life has a way of keeping us so busy that we seldom have time for all we wish to do, we never missed one of the fellowships to which we were invited. We also enjoyed getting to meet you and Matt and the rest of your family."

"Thank you Rachel. That is so kind of you to say. Caleb....all of us....enjoy the company of those who place family and integrity and living a godly life as their top priorities, like you and Richard do," Sarah said. "We all trust in these attributes and admire them. I also know that Caleb takes pride in the achievements of your children as they mirror your example to them. By the way, congratulations on your daughter's acceptance into medical school, it must be such a nice compliment when a child wants to follow in the footsteps of the parent."

"Yes," Rachel replied, "We were...are so proud of her and with five daughters, we hope to see each one of them find a vocation they love and then want to be the best they can be. Richard is like that....he is right on top of every medical break-through and always wants the best for his patients. He isn't content unless he gives his all."

"Thank you Rachel, for your kindness. I am so relieved that Richard is with Caleb at the hospital. Thinking about the damage that such a fall can do, I am guessing that Caleb may have some broken bones and if so, Richard as an orthopedic surgeon is the perfect person to help. I am so grateful that he is at the hospital...and even that he may be able to direct the family to the best physicians for any other type of injury. God is so good and often blesses us through other people."

"I've felt that way too Sarah because so often we seemed to have been directed to just the right people at the right time. We can think of it as a coincidence, but as these "co-incidents" mount in our lives, we look at them differently, and can begin to see them as a blessing."

"Yes....my grandmother always told us to look for God's blessings. She said that so many people go through life blinded to what occurs in their life, never giving credit to God and never realizing that there is a higher power or that we have a Heavenly Father who looks after us. For me, even when I was at the lowest point in my life, I *later* understood why God had allowed it. I saw that what had occurred was a mercy rather than a heartache. That recognition finally allowed me to let go and let God."

"Sometimes I wonder Sarah, if we can ever give our children all the wisdom they will require in life. It's scary to think that they will have to go through situations which are difficult and that what we as parents have taught them....or *not* taught them....will influence how they handle those situations."

"That's a great point Rachel. Sadly so few parents really 'teach'....they don't seem to understand how important it is to their children's future. I mean....we suffer as parents when our children suffer, so why not try to ease their suffering with some of the tips we learned to use ourselves? Whether it is faith in God, the value of personal accountability, or service to others, we need these things in our life to gain the self esteem to make something of ourselves. And I am not talking about money, but of what lives in someone's heart, what makes someone a valued friend, a role model, a person of integrity."

"We also need to teach our children when to run!" Rachel quipped, "There are some in the world who will provide the wrong influence and drag them down. Sometimes it's hard for children to recognize or to accept that. That can worry a parent too."

The phone rang then and Matt told Sarah that her brother Josh had phoned and would soon be dropping Debbie and their son Johnny at Ann's house so that Debbie could look after the children and Sarah could accompany Josh to the hospital. He also told her that they would speak to the physicians soon to get an update on Caleb's condition.

Rachel left so that Sarah would be ready to go when Debbie and Josh arrived. She told Sarah that she would check in again tomorrow to see if there was anything she could do for them. Sarah thanked her for coming and for her gift of friendship. Then Sarah checked the children once again and, satisfied that they still slept soundly, went to brew a pot of coffee for Deb and made enough to fill a thermos to bring to Ann, Matt, Preacher and Joe. When Deb and Josh arrived with one year old Johnny, Sarah had already poured them both a mug of coffee and had placed on the open counter between the kitchen and family room the Stevia sweeteners and the soy creamer they enjoyed with their coffee. While Sarah and Josh sat at the counter, Deb took Johnny into another of the spare bedrooms where she tucked him in to sleep. After checking on the other children, Andrew, Lorraine and Jason, Debbie joined them in the family room.

"Caleb is always so careful Sarah, so it's hard to imagine him falling off the roof."

"Josh, it was pouring rain and evidently something went awry with a delivery and when Caleb went to the roof to make sure the error was corrected, the safety harness he'd worn evidently failed to work properly. I don't know all the details, but just hope that Caleb will be okay."

"Yeah, well when we get to the hospital let's hope we can learn more. Maybe by then the docs will have explained to Ann and Matt exactly what injuries Caleb has sustained."

"When something like this happens, it really makes us appreciate the good health we experience each day.....we can lose it at any time." As Deb joined her husband and sister-in-law she added, "Accidents and ill health can turn one's life upside down and every plan you've made for your future can suddenly fall by the wayside......but we also see how we pull together as a family to help!"

Chapter Four

SATAN DOESN'T GIVE UP

Ann's head was swimming. She could not digest what the internist was trying to tell them. The words were so foreign to her that she could not understand what they meant nor how they related to Caleb. *What did it mean to "bruise" an organ? Why did they have to "wait and see" in regard to Caleb's head injury? What was the cartilage between the femur and tibia?* Ann understood that the doctor was talking about Caleb's injuries, but what did she know about these things? She asked the doctor to wait one moment before continuing and fumbled in her purse for a pen and notepaper. She explained that she wanted to write some of these words down so she could later look them up and understand their relationship to what Caleb would be facing.

Sensing her difficulty, the internist explained in simpler terms that there were three areas of concern; one was that the intensity of the fall had "shaken" some of Caleb's organs, causing them to bruise. "This should heal by itself without much intervention. Similarly, Caleb's head injury seems to indicate that we should wait and see rather than intervene at this time. However", he said while using Ann's notepad to draw a small diagram to indicate how the knee cartilage lay between the two legs bones. "Caleb may require knee surgery once his other systems heal."

"But what does all this mean", Ann asked? "How does all this impact Caleb? Will he be okay once all these things are fixed? Why did you say that you will have to 'wait and see' in terms of his head injury? Is it because he still isn't conscious? ......Why haven't I been allowed to see him? ....I need to see him.....When can I see him?"

"Ann, you can see him in a few minutes. He is undergoing a few more tests and while they are taking place, the neurologist and orthopedic surgeon will speak with you. I am going to cautiously tell you that I believe that Caleb will be okay. He's young and strong and healthy. But with head injuries and a possible coma, there is always the unexpected. But overall Ann, we think he should pull through this. There is a team of specialists assessing Caleb's various injuries as we speak. We still have a number of tests to perform and thereby a number of assessments to make, but all in all, given that the head injury does not get any worse, it looks as if Caleb will be okay. But.....it will take time. There are just a few more tests to perform and when the results are interpreted we can prognosticate with some accuracy. As soon as he's back in his room, you can see him."

Ann thanked the internist and looked at Matt as if wanting him to say something. There was so much to absorb and still she felt as if she was far from learning all that Caleb would face. Just as they sat once again, the neurologist came into the room, introduced himself and began to explain what he had learned about Caleb's condition.

"Caleb's brain was shaken by the impact of his fall. The membranes of the brain are very sensitive and consist of three separate entities. The dura matter is a dense material lining the interior of the skull, the archnoid membrane surrounds the nerves, and the pia mater is a vascular membrane. When swelling occurs, such as was produced by Caleb's fall, it can interfere with the normal function of the brain by preventing messages from being sent to the spinal column and out to the various parts of the body. Similarly, the spinal column, through which these nerves travel, must be able to receive and send the messages which the brain relays to them. Some of these instructions are automatic meaning that we are unaware of them, like for instance, breathing or when hormones are released. Others are processes of which we *are* aware such as talking or typing. My job is to reduce the swelling of the brain to allow and promote the activities which the brain performs. The brain wants to "talk to" the rest of the body so that all its functions will continue to work in a normal and optimal fashion. In most cases, this swelling lasts only a short while and reduces without much fanfare. In some cases, it occurs because of a formation of blood which must be removed. And sometimes it produces a coma which may also resolve by itself. We've found that if our tests show no reason to intervene, it is best to wait and see. This is what we are going to do with Caleb. Wait and see for another day or two as we closely monitor him. I'll be here most of the night and will check back with you if anything changes."

Ann and Matt thanked the doctor and sat down again. Sarah walked into the waiting room at that moment along with Josh, so Matt and Ann began to fill them in about what they just learned from the internist and the neurologist. Sarah and Josh had brought a huge thermos of coffee for everyone knowing that the hospital coffee was not as good as they could make at home. Everyone welcomed the coffee which was already flavored with their favorite Stevia and soy creamer. Ann welcomed the warmth which the cup of steaming coffee provided to her ice cold fingers.

Sarah told Ann that Rachel had visited soon after she and Joe had left for the hospital and about Richard's immediate run to the hospital when learning about Caleb. Ann was very grateful for her neighbor's concern and assistance. She and Caleb liked Rachel and Richard very much and trusted them implicitly. Ann knew that Caleb would be in good hands if Richard had anything to say about it!

"Maybe this will turn out okay after all", Ann thought. *"Maybe Caleb will need some minor surgery and then be okay again. Maybe I have simply allowed my mind to exaggerate this entire situation and thus allowed Satan to harm the faith I should have been exercising."*

Joe actually said aloud almost the same words which had filled Ann's thoughts: "I hate to admit this, knowing how religious and all you guys are.....but I sure got mad at God for allowing this to happen. But maybe Caleb will be okay and I got mad for nothing. Now I feel guilty."

"Joe," Josh said, "You are such a caring guy so you getting mad at God because you love Caleb is understandable....not only to me....but also to God. It's mind boggling to me that you *think* you don't 'believe'....I think you do!"

"Ha, me? No way.....I mean....I guess that there is a god and all......but well, why would He bother with me....I mean why would He care about everything I do…gosh….think for a minute….have you ever calculated the number of people who have lived on earth……and you can still say He's cared about them all?"

"Yeah, we do!" Matt replied. "God does and has cared for *every* soul who ever lived, was ever conceived or ever died. Time doesn't matter for Him! In fact our time is only determined by our sun and moon which God created to measure our progress. However, there *is* no time or limit to or for God! In fact, it wasn't until the *end of the fourth day* according to Genesis that God even created the sun and moon in order to produce time as we know it. Before then, there *was* no time….certainly not as we measure it today."

"Waddya mean Matt, that for four days of the *seven* days when God was creating the other parts of this world, there was *no* time?"

"Right! Time was indefinite in those first four "days" so "evolution" could easily have occurred. Carbon dating fits perfectly into what the Bible tells us about the Creation. With the hundreds of thousands of years before mankind, why should the 6,000 years we have existed be difficult for God, why *couldn't* He have been active in all those lives?"

"Well, that time thing is news to me. Lemme think about that one. But still.....even 6.000 years is a long time in my book to have the patience to put up with so many generations of people and all the sin and anger and hate and war and cruelty and just plain stupidity."

"Not if God created a specific time frame during which just so many people would be born and have the opportunity to learn of Him, of His plan for mankind, learn to love Him, and want to follow Him." Josh added. "In fact, the Bible tells us that though God wants *all* men to be saved, not all men *will* be saved thus not all will enter the new heaven and earth He plans to create."

Just as Sarah was about to add to the conversation, Richard walked into the waiting room and greeted them. He knew everyone...including Preacher and Joe who'd often been at Ann and Caleb's fellowships.

"Hello everyone. I am so sorry that we have to meet under these circumstances. Rachel and I have always enjoyed our visits with you all, and I wish that could be what we are doing today. But.....we have to face the facts and deal with what we have been given. Ann, are you holding up okay?"

"I guess I am Richard....I'm just scared....I need to know that Caleb will be okay."

"Well, I've looked at some of the preliminary tests and it looks as if both knees are damaged beyond repair. The damage will cause one of the two bones in the lower leg and the one in the upper leg to rub against one another which then causes a lot of pain and further damage to those bones. Caleb will need surgery to replace the damaged areas. The surgery is routine but it's a rough recovery requiring hard work and determination.

Now....the physicians who are caring for Caleb's other injuries, are....cautiously....optimistic. We will wait and see but we don't think that we will find anything more than we already have. There's some bruising on various organs, so we'll watch that carefully.....but...all in all his accident could have been a lot worse. Once we feel that Caleb is free of soft tissue damage and free of any trauma to the bones, and is fully functional again, we can operate on his knees."

When Matt asked for more detail about knee replacement surgery, Richard put his two fists together using his knuckles to demonstrate how the lower part of the upper leg bone contains two rounded protrusions which move in conjunction with the two plateaus on the upper end of the larger bone below the knee. "This movement is cushioned by the cartilage between these bones. However, Caleb's cartilage can no longer do that job, therefore will result in bone damage, in escalating pain and eventually, an inability to walk. Replacement surgery will, through a prosthetic device, provide a new surface to both these bones and replace the cartilage between them."

"Thanks Richard. We have the utmost trust in you and I thank you for not glossing over his injuries but are willing to tell us exactly what you found. We need that and we want that. It allows us to rest assured that Caleb is in good hands. Thanks so much for being such a good friend. But Richard…I know Caleb and so do you. He is not going to take kindly to any absence from work. That mall project is huge in scope but also huge in his mind as a stepping stone to so many of the things he's wanted for our family. I am worried about what his state of mind will be."

"Ann, I can't predict that. All I can say is that we will watch carefully to determine how he's doing… all around....body, mind and spirit....and be there to support him and to guide him to all the professional help he might require....also covering body, mind and spirit. With the support of a family like yours, you won't have to worry.....he will be okay even if the road seems rocky from time to time. Come on Ann, now let me see that pretty smile!"

Ann didn't feel like smiling....she knew that a long recovery period was going to be a huge problem for Caleb...but she smiled anyway and tried not to allow her true feelings to show. Richard however, had noted the depth of Ann's concerns and guessed that both she and Caleb would have to fight many a negative emotion. There was a lot at stake here given Caleb's investment in the property next to the mall.....and in today's world...who knew what an employer would do? Richard thought to himself....*Well, I'll keep this in mind and watch carefully for the "if and when". They might need some additional support for the emotional aspect of a long recovery.* He liked this family and he respected the way they lived their life and cared for one another. He grinned at Ann saying, "Let's go see Caleb!"

Joe, Matt, Sarah, Josh, Preacher and Joe remained in the waiting room and sat in a semi-circle. They began to talk about what they had just learned about Caleb.

"This is not going to be easy for Caleb, not only physically, but emotionally." Matt said. "He's taken such a big gamble by purchasing that acreage near the mall and is now very dependent on his salary from the mall project. Joe...Preacher...do either of you know how these giant corporations react when it comes to this stuff......I mean in terms of disability or worker's comp? It's my thought that these benefits do not provide a complete pay check do they?"

"You know Matt, I really don't know", Joe replied. "But we should find out because if they do, then Caleb won't be so worried. And maybe we can also ask Richard if Caleb can still supervise from a wheelchair or something after just a few weeks. If so, then the company could keep him on the job and pay him his full salary. Caleb is always jumping in and helping the men, but really, that's not his job description, so why not stick to the supervising end? Disability does not cover your entire pay...I know that much....but Workman's Compensation might be different."

"I know that the healing is most important, but let's face it, the financial end will be a worry for Ann and Caleb, so it would be great if we could alleviate these concerns by getting more information about these benefits. Maybe it's too early for the docs to make a time commitment regarding how long Caleb will be out of work because they don't yet know the extent of Caleb's injuries or how quickly he might heal."

"Come on guys, now is the time for faith......a time for prayer.... not conjecture and worry", Sarah interjected. "We seem to be caught up in the secular or material parts of our lives instead of thanking God that Caleb is alive and *can* be healed. Frankly, I am a little disappointed in these conversations. What's happened to us...to trusting God...to accepting where He leads us? This isn't right!"

"Now Sarah, wait a minute" Josh added, "We've been praying....but sometimes we also have to consider the practical side of things don't we? Isn't there a fine line between just sitting back and doing nothing and getting to work to help ourselves and one another....and trusting God to direct our ways and the outcomes of those interventions which *we* must initiate? Isn't there a saying that God helps those who help themselves?"

"Well, you're right Josh", Sarah added, "but we have to put God first and be careful not to let Satan bring a lot of negativity into our discussions...especially when Ann is present......she's worried....about Caleb of course, but also because she, as a mother, feels responsible for her children's welfare. She and Caleb took a big risk to buy that property and I am sure that it will work out because Caleb out a lot of prayer into making that decision and we have to watch that Satan doesn't break our faith and our trust in God. We need to be careful."

Joe broke into the conversation saying, "This Satan fella.....I don't get it. Are you saying that he can control all that stuff.....like your mind....your finances.....your life? I mean, come on....that's not possible. *We* control our minds and our life don't we? And isn't God supposed to help us do that?"

"It's complicated Joe" Matt explained. "But here's an explanation in a nutshell. Satan and God are at war and we are the prize over which they fight. Here's how this all started: Satan was an angel in heaven named Lucifer who became incredibly jealous when God created man and told those in heaven that He planned to raise mankind higher than the angels. Lucifer, angry at this announcement rebelled and made war against God. He convinced one third of all the angels to join his rebellion. God cast them from heaven to earth where Satan began to harass mankind and cause them to sin by being disobedient to God. By keeping man from God, Satan calculated that God would reign over the angels left in heaven while he would reign, *with equal power,* over mankind here on earth. But God sent His Son to earth as a ransom to pay for the sins of man which would allow them to be redeemed. Through Christ mankind again could turn back to Him, follow His precepts and be found worthy. However, because of man's sin, God's righteousness and the free will He gave mankind *required* Him to allow Satan to work to convince man to follow him and not follow God. Thus, Satan fights to keep us from trusting God and God fights to help us believe. When God finds the number of souls He wants for His new kingdom, Satan will be bound forever. This is the battle we are in and we are the prize!"

"And we don't even know this?" Joe asked.

"No….unless we've read the Bible, believe what God tells us through scripture, and decide to live as God asks us to live." Josh added. "We then begin to recognize when Satan attacks and when God redeems."

"I still can't understand why everyone doesn't know this stuff. I mean, if this *is* all true, why isn't it taught in school or in every church… or in books or something?"

"Joe, it is taught in books, in the Bible, in Sunday schools, in churches, and everyone *should* know this…..but when just one parent closes their mind and then doesn't teach their children who in turn don't teach their children, it becomes lost information. And this is exactly what Satan wants! If mankind doesn't *know* what's at stake, they won't worry about it…and Satan remains free!"

At that moment, Ann returned…a frantic Ann….tears running down her face, hands shaking, saying "Caleb has spiked a fever and has had a convulsion."

Matt, Josh and Sarah looked at one another and mouthed the words, "Satan doesn't give up".

Chapter Five

WHY GOD WHY?

Ann had been sent home from the hospital to see the children, rest, shower, and change her clothes. Before leaving, she'd seen Caleb again and had been assured that he was resting peacefully and had responded to the medications he'd been given. This had given her a temporary respite and she'd fought hard to believe that from this point on, Caleb would be alright. She sent Debbie home after thanking her for her help. After playing a while with the children, she took the shower she'd longed for, and as the children played, she sat at the kitchen table with a cup of tea. Her mind inspected her relationship with God. She felt bereft, believing that she'd failed God. Even with the understanding that feeling anger about what had happened was wrong, she couldn't help thinking the worst; she couldn't stop her thoughts and didn't *want* to stop her anger. She didn't trust enough to accept the terrible circumstances which could arise as a result of Caleb's accident. She knew that her attitude disappointed God and that she'd failed an important test of faith; failed as a child of God. *Given the hundreds of miracles of faith I have experienced, why is it that when I am tested, my faith falls apart? Do others go through this, too?*

She placed her arms on the counter where she sat and laid her head on her arms and began to cry. *Am I just supposed to give up everything we've worked for the way Abraham gave up the son he loved when God tested him? Am I supposed to be like Job who just accepted all his losses?*

She began to wonder how Abraham could have picked up the knife and been ready to take Isaac's life. She didn't think that she could *ever* have that much faith. She was sure that with the attitude she had at this moment, she could *never* be found worthy. Guilt, self-accusation and hopelessness filled her heart even as she understood that it was Satan who placed those thoughts and emotions there.

A bit later, Elizabeth arrived to look after the children and was saddened to find Ann crying. In her loving, motherly way she took Ann into her arms and asked Ann to tell her what was bothering her. Ann, usually so reticent, blurted everything out, telling Elizabeth of how she had failed God and failed her family. Elizabeth tried to comfort her.

"Ann, forgiving ourselves is an important step toward learning how to forgive others. We aren't perfect. And....unfortunately we *are* subject to the thoughts Satan plants in our minds until we recognize them. God knows this, and knows that this is part of our learning process. If our hearts are right, and we seek God and love Him, we *do* learn.... and over *time* we change: we trust, we grow. Much of our pain and fear is wrapped around our pride....meaning those things....right or wrong.... by which we define ourselves."

"Don't be so hard on yourself, Ann. You are still in shock and in time, you will come to grips with all the thoughts and worries this situation has brought to you. God will give you time to understand and….He will help you learn why He has allowed this to occur and what good will come of it. I too went through some of these same feelings when my husband died and then again when I thought that I might die and leave Rebecca alone in the world. It was then that I learned about the 49 verses in scripture which contain the word pride. Each of these verses condemn pride as an attitude displeasing to God and defiling to man. Webster's Dictionary defines the word pride as "inordinate self-esteem, conceit, delight or elation with a position, possession or relationship, disdainful, and haughty". Roget's Thesaurus lists the words "egotism", "arrogant" and "regarding oneself with undue favor" as synonyms. I was shocked to read these definitions and was forced to think about the many reasons why we develop pride."

"This concept frightened me and made me feel unworthy of God's love. So, I decided to try to understand what pride really consists of and whether or not I was as guilty of it. I concluded that usually pride exists because of an asset we project to others such as beauty, intelligence, wealth, talent, power, position or eloquent speech. Ironically, these are blessings from God, not something we can conjure up by ourselves. Being proud of an accomplishment toward which we labored and for which we thank God is very different than exhibiting pride to exalt ourselves above others, *even if only in our own mind!*"

"As I read the verses in scripture which address pride, I saw that in most of them God warns us that those who feel or exhibit this pride will be brought down. Isaiah 25:11 tells us *"And......he shall bring down their pride together with the spoils of their hands."* Daniel 5:20 warns, *"But when .....his mind hardened in pride, he was deposed from his kingly throne...."* Obadiah 2-4 tells us, *"Behold......The pride of thy heart hath deceived thee....though thou exalt thyself as the eagle....I bring thee down saith the Lord."*

"What this means is that we will have to determine whether or not we truly want to place God first in our lives, recognize that all we are and have comes from Him and become willing to take a blow to our pride...humble ourselves to do so. Despite the foolishness of man and his fall from grace, God always gives us a second chance for redemption; a second chance to change our ways by learning His words, and from those words, also learn how we are to conduct ourselves, and.... learn what is pleasing or displeasing to Him. God graciously forgives our mistakes once we recognize them and try...strive.... to correct them."

"But if we nurture the evil which brings pride and arrogance into our lives, and do not know or heed God's words, the day will come when we can be overwhelmed by this spirit, no longer obtain grace, and may lose our soul salvation. It is the lowly and the humble God will mold."

"Yes Elizabeth, you're right. I remember reading in the book of Proverbs, some comprehensive instruction about pride and how it will impact our spiritual life. Proverbs says that pride is a spirit which is evil and must be exorcized from our heart. Specifically, Proverbs 16:18 tells us: *"Pride goweth before destruction...."* Proverbs 8:13 says, *"The.....Lord.....hate...pride, and arrogancy......"* Proverbs 11:2 tells us, *"When pride cometh, then cometh shame...."* Proverbs 29:23 warns, *"A man's pride shall bring him low...."*

"Exactly, Ann. Zephaniah tells us that pride is from a "god of the earth". Mark 7:20-23 tells us: *"....That which cometh out of the man.....pride....defile the man."* All the warnings about pride can be summed up in two verses, one from 1 John, and another from 1 Timothy. The verse from 1 John 2:16 says: "*.... the pride of life, is not of the Father, but is of the world.*" The verse from 1 Timothy 3:6 warns, "*....lest being lifted up with pride he fall into the condemnation of the devil.*" Sadly, we rarely recognize our pride.

"There are also a number of passages throughout scripture which provide insight into the progress we make as children of God. They are benchmarks by which we can gauge our progress toward becoming an overcomer and help us understand what we have, have not, can and cannot accomplish. But what we forget is that without being humbled...often....we would not be brought back to the reality of our personal and deadly failings. Scripture tells us that not only are we sinners, but that our hearts are evil."

"Despite our struggles to become more Christ-like in nature, we fall far from that goal and can only make changes in our lives through Our Heavenly Father and by the grace He has provided through Christ. 1 Corinthians 12:7-11 tells us that even the Apostle Paul had to be reminded of his fallibility. The Apostle Paul asked God to remove the "thorn" from his side and God answered by telling him to bear the thorn because God's grace would be sufficient to cover it. It was this "thorn" or "failing" which kept the Apostle Paul humble; kept reminding him that he was imperfect, and kept foremost in his mind that without God's intervention ad forgiveness he could never be found worthy. And Paul was then thankful for it!"

Ann's tears stopped as she began to understand what she might need to learn and she said, "I remember Elizabeth that scripture also tells us that what we see as a great fault in others often pales in comparison to our own faults. Matthew 7:3-5 explains that there may be a speck in the eye of someone with whom we find fault and a beam in our own. Yet our human nature fights against acknowledging that this could be true. We....I..... easily minimize, rationalize and justify our ....my faults, and maximize the faults in others. But now I can see that the beauty of our faith is that once we begin to acknowledge our faults we begin to change. God, out of His incredible love for us, allows us to stumble and even occasionally make fools of ourselves, so that we will experience embarrassment, sadness, remorse or even anger... but we are then forced to acknowledge our imperfections. This weakens the pride which is so damaging to our soul."

"That's true Ann, when children witness the actions of those who are quick to acknowledge their mistakes, quick to forgive mistakes in others, and quick to give praise to God in all things, they learn... at an early age... those things which others struggle for many years to learn. Children are our future and sadly many are not being taught about Satan nor what God wants us to learn. Children learn pride from prideful parents and learn humbleness by watching their parents remain humble."

"It's natural to take pride in our home, our job, our spouse, our children....and God does not frown upon such pride as long as we never allow it to supersede His will for our lives. Job lost *everything* he'd worked so hard to attain, the Prodigal son lost everything he'd inherited, the rich man was told to give up his riches, Abraham was asked to give up the one thing in life he'd longed for......but in the end God *didn't* take from them....in the end God blessed them because in their hearts they were able to let it go.... Simply because *God asked it of them.*"

"But Elizabeth, how can I do this? How can I stop asking myself why God would allow such calamity into such a good man's life? Caleb is in pain, he's hurt, he may take a very long time to recover, he may lose everything he's worked for......and I am to not worry, not be concerned, not ask God why?"

"No Ann, you are to communicate *all* your feelings to God, the good ones *and* the bad ones. Then you are to let Him know that you are sorry for the bad thoughts and ask Him to help you overcome them *and to trust Him.* Praying this way builds a sort of protective wall around you so that these thoughts can't impact you the way that Satan intends for them to impact you. In fact, if you do this, your whole attitude will change and you will become a more positive force for Caleb. God wants you to demonstrate your allegiance to Him by trusting Him *with* Caleb....with you and the children too."

"Oh Elizabeth, do you think I can do this? I want so much to do the right thing...it's just that I don't know how! And....and well, it just seems so unfair and difficult to do."

"That's understandable Ann. That's why God is teaching you. We are not *born* knowing how to please God. We have to grow into it. We have to learn, have to see what is evil by experiencing evil and what is good by experiencing what is good....then decide through our free will... which path we want to take. That decision is what can make of us a child of God. The easiest way for Satan to break our faith is to take something from us and push us into anger or despair over that loss. Whether rich or poor it is human nature to hate loss and wish for the return of what we had considered "ours". This attitude comes from the old Adam-like nature which Satan can affect, rather than the new godly nature which God wants us to develop."

"In fact we are often so arrogant that when we experience loss we actually *expect* that in time, with prayer, God will *return* what was taken from us. It is in these circumstances that our faith is severely tested and we must truly trust God so we *can* fully accept that loss. Accepting loss by laying our concerns into God's hands is a sure way to the blessing He wants to provide for us."

"Elizabeth, is this what happened to you when your husband died...when his cancer could not be cured."

"Yes Ann it did. In the end, it drew me closer to God and it brought me into Mary and Kevin's life, and ultimately into yours. So, it wasn't in vain and, I believe that I will be re-united with my husband one day and that God had his reasons not only for what transpired, but also for the *timing* of what transpired. Someone once told me that God takes us home when we have reached the highest spiritual point we can attain while we are here on earth rather than allow Satan to pull us down. That's a comforting thought. I do believe that my husband was at a wonderful spiritual peak when he died."

"I feel embarrassed to think that it's just my pride which causes my worry Elizabeth. It seems so selfish of me."

"Well, Ann….it is selfish….but it is a form of self-preservation. *The Adam-like nature must preserve itself because without God there is nothing else to preserve it. The Christ-like nature gives all away because it relies on God to care for it.* You are simply listening to your "Adam" rather than submitting to "Christ" and once you understand this phenomena you can make your own decision as to who you will *choose* to "listen" to! You are learning and developing as God wants you to. In fact, do you remember all the stories that Caleb, Sarah and Josh often tell about Grandma and how she used to yell the word "NO" aloud many times each day? She'd tell them that the birds of thoughts which she knew she should *not* entertain were flying over her head and she did not want them to roost so she was shooing them away."

"Ha, ha, yes I do remember that Elizabeth....so....you are telling me that I can make the decision about what I *want* to think and feel and ask God to help me... and that He will! And you are also telling me that I can *choose* to trust even if I will have to work on it? You're telling me to say "NO" when my thoughts become negative!"

"Exactly Ann! Now cheer up and begin practicing! In no time, you'll get the hang of it and you'll see God working in your life....and even if it's not quite the way you had envisioned, in time it will be so much *greater* than your own ideas."

"Thanks Elizabeth, I really do feel better now. I have a lot to think about and a lot of practicing to do! And, now that you are here for the children, I'd think that I should get back to the hospital. You are such a Godsend. Thank you!"

"Honey, God will always find a way to comfort us whether it is through a person, a book, a movie, a church service, a T.V. show…it doesn't matter…..but always He is there, teaching us, helping us. We just have to be open to Him when He does come to us with loving instruction!"

With a happy heart for the first time in many hours Ann kissed the children, hugged Elizabeth, grabbed her purse and didn't ask the question '*Why God Why*'?

Chapter Six

THE STRUGGLE TO OVERCOME

It was about six weeks later when Caleb was finally medically cleared to have his knee surgery. Richard was explaining the general procedure for knee replacement surgery and what Caleb could expect in terms of both the surgery itself and the recovery. "The surgery will take about two hours....maybe a bit longer if I find more damage than I anticipate. You will be given a spinal for the anesthesia so should have no adverse reaction when you awaken. I am very careful to cauterize as I move along so always hope for minimal blood loss....however, there is blood loss, sometimes even the need for a blood transfusion, although it's rare that my patients require one. We can treat any mild anemia after the surgery. Caleb, I have to warn you....it's not the surgery but the rehab which is difficult for the patient. It's a lot of work, it takes perseverance, it's painful, it's time consuming and it's easy to slip back if you do not follow through on the exercises."

"You said "time consuming"....how much time Richard?"

"Well, a lot depends on your physical condition before surgery, on your dedication to performing the recommended exercises even above and beyond the rehabilitation procedures, *and* the ability of your body to heal. I'll say that for you, in three months you'll be getting around on your own and in six months to a year you'll be doing everything you did before the accident. But, sometimes it can even take two years before you are as good as new. You can have your second knee done one or two months or so after the first, so you can add a little more time for that."

"I can't take that long....I have to work....I have to complete the mall.....I can't lose this job."

"Caleb, listen to me....I can most likely approve you for work on a very limited basis.....but once you have the surgery you cannot take the risk of damaging what we repaired or you'll be back to square one. I'll have to know what you need to do at work, what type of ground surfaces you'll have to navigate upon and any potential danger these might offer, what positions you'll keep your knees in, and for how long...and... when you'll get in all the rehab which I will *require* you to do."

"But Richard, you don't understand....if they replace me at work.....if they think I won't be back right away....well I don't know what will happen."

"Let's find out before we make any decisions. Let's talk to your boss and ask him if there are any guidelines which he will have to follow. This is, after all, a case for workman's compensation and/or disability for a short while, I'd think. So before you jump in, let's get some facts."

"Yeah, I guess you're right." Caleb replied, "but is there any reason why you can't do both knees at the same time?"

"I have done both at once, but not on a regular basis and it is not what I generally recommend. The risks are greater. There is more blood loss, a longer time spent under the anesthesia, it is more traumatic to your body, and it is a more difficult recovery…..all things you must consider."

"I want both knees done at the same time Richard so I can get back to normal as quickly as I can, and it makes medical sense because both knees are damaged, therefore putting weight on the bad knee because the new knee will hurt is sort of an oxymoron! Am I right?"

"Alright Caleb, you win! Sometimes you are too smart for your own good! But promise me that you'll always level with me. I've seen cases where a state of mind can interfere with recovery. Your desire to heal quickly is commendable but sometimes healing simply requires time. Additionally, pushing yourself too much can result in compromising the healing process and causing more physical pain. This can result in emotional pain which adds to what you already have to bear. While we usually seem to accept physical pain as normal in certain circumstances, we tend to feel guilty when we express emotional pain. So I want you to talk to me, be open with me, okay?"

"Richard, I've been lying here in this bed for weeks already and I think about what scripture tells us in Romans 8:28, *"All things work together for the good of those that love the Lord."* Therefore I've been trying to wear a happy face regardless of how I *really* feel. But I *know*, just somehow *know* that I should have both knees done at once. And Richard, I understand that the children of God can expect Satan to bring us our heartache, physically, emotionally and spiritually, and that our Heavenly Father in His loving kindness and the righteousness under which He works, promises to turn those heartaches into a blessing. I also believe that our Heavenly Father has ordained that, because of sin, our lives have become our training ground whereby we learn how to become all that God hopes us to become. Therefore He allows our difficult circumstances to become *a marker of our character development* and the readiness which is required of those who will become the Bride He wants for His Son."

"But Caleb, let's be honest here. There are times when we live through heartache or witness the heartache of those we love and we ask ourselves privately how this promise of good from all circumstances could be possible. While we believe that scripture is God's personal, accurate and irrefutable instruction, seldom do we think to ask Him to unravel the mystery attached to His words and help us recognize their miracle and internalize how they are to be utilized. We suffer in silence and do not admit that inwardly we rail at what we face and then feel guilty about our private thoughts. The return of the happiness we have attached to what was or might be lost becomes not only our new hope, but also our expectation. Yet *the truth may be that what we want is not good for us or for those we love."*

"Richard, I agree, really I do.......people argue that they've been relatively good and faithful and will now become even better people and more faithful in the future and therefore, God being all powerful, should help them *by restoring* what they have lost. As they lose patience with waiting or begin to think that this time they may *not* obtain restoration, they immediately blame God and wonder why He has not helped, even when He has provided them with an answer....which they may not like! What they may have forgotten is that Satan is alive and well and his goal is to break their faith. I won't let this happen to me."

"Yeah, but many may forget that the reward God promises His children may come only after great sacrifice, after being tried in the fire and with accepting God's will. This can cause us to direct the anger and impatience we feel toward God and not toward Satan or toward what *we* ourselves might be lacking. It is a terrible thing to suffer and to see that what we have worked for, hoped for, took for granted or expected, has suddenly disappeared and seems to be irreversibly gone. It is even more difficult when those who depend upon us also must suffer from our loss. Sometimes we *must* ask God "Why?""

"But Richard, isn't it because as we move through our times of despair we must strive to believe that God is with us and that we can trust Him to bring us through the difficulty we face and then to accept His will for our circumstance? But to do this, we have to have a certain amount of peace in our hearts to function properly. Peace is a precious commodity and while most of us try to preserve the peace we have, sometimes we falter and our troubles remove the peace from our hearts."

"You're right Caleb, but I want you to think this over carefully. Our patience is often limited and our good intentions don't always pan out. If you want both knees done at the same time, I'll do it, but you have to think about how hard this might be for you….and Ann."

"Richard, scripture tells us that both our Heavenly Father and His Son offer us their peace when we need help. Philippians 4:19 says: ""*And the peace of God…. shall keep your hearts and minds…..*" And* John 14:27 tells us that Christ said: *"Peace I leave with you, my peace I give unto you…… Let not your heart be troubled, neither let it be afraid."* But what should we do when we lose our strength and our peace? And why do we lose it? Scripture tells us that Satan attacks the children of God and that he knows *where* we are the most vulnerable. We also learn from scripture that God allows Satan to attack us because during that attack we have the opportunity to grow in faith and be refined in the process. God would not offer strength if He did not know we would need it. And even though I know that Philippians 4:13 assures us: *"I can do all things through Christ which strengtheneth me.",* this is my family at stake, my livelihood, our future and so I have to put my trust in God to make it work."

"Well Caleb, I have respected you for many things…. one of which is your faith. It's beautiful and it's admirable. Perhaps now is *your* test and though I know you *can* do it, I just hope that you really will just let go, as you have often told others, and let God. You're human too ya know!"

"Yeah, I know. That's the hard part. Talk is cheap! But I am counting on the fact that once Satan sees that we understand what is occurring and sees that our heart is filled with thankfulness for the very thing which Satan thought would destroy us, he'll *leave*. He'll know that he lost that battle! I am *trying* to accept and to trust. I am really appalled that I am struggling with this. I know what scripture says about the expression of the fear, or pain, or sorrow we experience. In fact it is best understood as we examine what Christ lived through and what He felt and expressed. His reaction is our example. Christ spoke the words, *"Take away this cup from me"*, which clearly demonstrates that He did not want to go through what He knew He had to face. He asked God *not to ask* Him to endure what He knew was to be a terrible experience. While my pain cannot begin to emulate the pain Christ endured for us, I think that Christ's experience teaches me not to feel guilty if I ask God to change my circumstances. But I will try to learn from the love in the heart of Christ and the trust He had in His Father. That love allowed Christ to submit to His sacrifice for us and it produced the character in His soul which caused Him to utter the words,

"Nevertheless, not what I will, but what thou will" ....after asking for it to be removed."

"This will be my example Richard. It shows me that God certainly allows us to express our fear, the pain we feel, and to express our wish that our circumstances were different. It is not that we are judged and found lacking when we *ask* God to take our troubles away, but that we end up *accepting* God's will and doing our best to *use* those circumstances to prove our character."

"Everything you say Caleb is true. Our troubles will then become an indicator of the trust and acceptance which lives in our heart for the decisions of our Heavenly Father....no matter what the circumstances are. *How* we handle our troubles becomes, in essence, a marker of our spiritual maturity and our spiritual character. The miracle which occurs when we *adjust* our thoughts and actions, as Christ did when facing His heartrending circumstances, is that once we submit to God's will, our heartaches often become easier to bear, or simply disappear. Especially if we accept the adjustment or learn the lesson which is intended."

"Once Satan realizes that he cannot break our faith, nor break our trust, there is no reason for him to continue his harassment. We then, are not only often *released* from Satan's captivity, but are also wiser and more trustworthy for having mastered the test which God arranged these circumstances to bring us."

"Yes Richard, you're right and it certainly is difficult to experience heartache whether it comes from the death of a child, a debilitating disease, devastating betrayal, or watching someone we love suffer....or facing what I now face. In fact, I can remember examining Christ's plea that God remove the cup from which He was to drink, and then His words of submission. I began to understand what this effort cost Him. When we understand what Christ endured, and better appreciate His sacrifice, our own suffering is so much less because we recognize that it benefits us and perhaps those we love. Mark 14:34 tells us of the emotional pain Christ suffered when we read Christ's words: *"My soul is exceedingly sorrowful unto death."* What few of us realize is that Christ later even repeated His plea that God would 'take away this cup from me' a second time. Asking a second time was indicative of how much He was suffering as he simply *thought* of what was to come. Mark 14:39 tells us, *"and again He went away and prayed, and spoke the same words."* Therefore, if we are caught up in a circumstance which seems to have no end, or to be unfair, we need not feel guilty when we ask God to let our circumstances pass, as long as our heart truly desires that God's will be paramount. This is indicative of the trust we place in God's design for our lives and perhaps the lives of those we love. Further, by trying to be more introspective and asking ourselves if we trust that which is occurring for our good, as scripture teaches, and ask whether or not we are willing to endure our circumstances in order to develop our character, we can grow into the Bride God desires for His Son. Once we reflect on these questions and ask our Heavenly Father to help us learn from everything we experience, we can move with all our heart and with great sincerity from the words *"Take this away"* to the words, *"Thy will be done"*. This allows God access to our hearts and the ability to create the change in us which we require."

"Yes Caleb, Christ dreaded the circumstances which He was to live through. He was afraid, He found Himself without any earthly support, and without a true and loyal friend. Christ's cup was a bitter one; it was the most bitter cup of circumstances any of us could ever imagine, yet because of His love for us, He stood firm and He trusted and obeyed what His Heavenly Father ordained."

"Richard, Satan threw everything he had against Christ, but Christ remained stedfast. Thus, the Bride of Christ must remain firm in her trust and obedience to God and bring her sorrow and fear to God with honesty. She can be assured that God loves her, sees her tears, carries her through all circumstances, and creates a blessing from them. Our character, which is comprised of our ability to love and forgive, to have compassion and understanding, to submit to God's will, to be loyal and to trust God implicitly, will be measured by how we deal with our circumstances. Those who have developed these attributes will be a part of the five wise, and not the five foolish virgins, and found worthy to go with the Lord when He takes His Bride. Our suffering, and our trials and tribulations, are for our greater good. How we handle them will be an example to those around us. How we approach adversity is a marker of our spiritual maturity. These are but a few of the blessings which God creates from our heartache and why all things work for the good of those who love the Lord."

"Caleb...hang onto all you have just told me. You have taken a good look at what you face and a good and realistic look at the fact that in the end you may have no job, no money and may even think for a little while that God does not hear you. But when we know God's words and take to heart the comfort of those words, we have defeated evil and we will have come through the fire. We can also be assured that soon God will bless us. Further, we know that we will never fall to a point where we cannot be lifted up again and be better for the experience. The story of Job shows us that God can restore all things and that if we remain faithful and trust Him He is bound in His righteousness to walk with us and carry us through all things."

"Richard…thanks for this conversation. I've talked too much I guess, but I think it's because I am worried that I might be someone who talks the talk and doesn't walk the walk. I'm scared….I'm afraid that I am not going to be all I should be. I'm not sure that I can do all the things we've talked about, but I sure do know that I *want* to. I think that I'm afraid for the times when I'll be fearful, when Ann and I will worry, when I might experience a lot of pain and be terribly impatient, maybe feel discouraged, maybe even angry. But if I can just draw again on this conversation, maybe I can do it….maybe I can hold on….maybe I can trust more that God will handle the outcome."

"Now that's the Caleb I know and love……and believe me, I'll remind you of this conversation when you start to complain!"

Chapter Seven

<u>SUCCESSES AND FAILURES</u>

Caleb was finally scheduled to have his bilateral knee surgery and when the anesthesiologist came to talk with him before the surgery, Caleb asked him if spinal anesthesia meant that he'd hear the saws shaving away at the edges of the four bones in his legs or hear the mallet which would rightly fit the prosthesis into those bones. "I'd rather not hear that Doc.....it seems so.....final. You know....it's like suddenly becoming aware that a part of you is disappearing. That doesn't make sense I guess, but can you keep me under?"

"Sure Caleb, we can do that with some meds which have a short term effect and can be administered through your IV. We'll be watching you carefully and you'll be just fine!"

"Thanks Doc......I guess I'm more of a baby than I thought!"

As he waited to be wheeled into the surgical suite, Caleb thought about work. None of his bosses wanted to talk about his job status until after the surgery. This worried him. *Were they just being kind or was the news going to be devastating to him?* Either way, by the end of the week he was sure to learn exactly what their plans were. He and Ann had talked about the times when a Christian finds himself laboring under a tremendous heartache which appears impossible to remedy. They discussed how difficult it is to reflect on one's faith when one has done everything they know how to do to please God and yet were *still* afraid. He had asked Ann what she thought about someone who might have labored to change whatever mistakes once governed their lives, yet the situation in which they found themselves did not change. After months or years of struggle; of doing their best to learn and practice God's words, and of praying for help, and no help appears to arrive, wouldn't it be a normal consequence for them to ask God why their circumstance did not change? Maybe they even ask where God is in their lives. Do these questions make them less a true Christian?

"I don't think so Caleb. God understands that Satan cleverly uses a sense of despair to rob a child of God of hope and faith, and capture them with a spirit of depression to prevent their faith from being active. But, what we *should* fear is that when we are about to be freed from one spirit, Satan will try to bind us with another. It is a classical part of spiritual warfare that when we are finally to overcome something which has been holding us back from becoming all that God sees in us, Satan brings us something else to keep us in captivity. Thus it can seem that we make no progress in our natural lives or in our spiritual lives. We have been so blessed not to have had to endure such continued hard times, yet those times are when we are tested and when we have the opportunity to prove our faith. We both have to try to uplift one another by talking about God's mercy and assuring one another that during these difficult times, huge changes are taking place which we can't yet see."

"Ann, what if we have been under the control of a spirit which we have not yet recognized or which requires a great deal of time to remove? If we desire to go back to the way things were before the start of our heartache, perhaps we'd never rid ourselves of that spirit. Maybe it's even related to the inherited sin which scripture tells us can be passed from generation to generation and we don't realize it. Maybe change takes time because God is preparing another person or event to direct a change in our circumstance. What we need to believe is that if God has brought us to a crossroad, and we strive to be faithful, He will see us through it and that He *always* brings a blessing from it. We....I.... just have to be patient. I am so thankful that our ministers visited and prayed with us and will continue to pray for us and our family. We not only need the support of family and friends but also the support of our bearers of blessing and fellow believers. God does know better than we what is good for us and while Satan may take something from us, God will allow it because *He can see* that what we had... would have, in time.... brought us harm and also harm our soul salvation. He promises to comfort us as we go through the trial of fire which Satan may have brought but which God will use to purify us and lead us to greener pastures. Matthew 11:28 does tell us: *"Come unto me, all ye that labour and are heavy laden, and I will give you rest."*

"Caleb, let's try hard.... especially when we feel exhausted from our struggle....to recall the comforting words of scripture. Let's try harder to trust that God will supply all our needs, even if they are supplied at the very last moment, or will not be in the time or fashion we expected. I love the words of Philippians 4:19: *"....God shall supply all your need".*

"I know that you are afraid for our future Ann, especially since we recently took on so much debt, but if all this is so we grow in faith, then let's try to joyfully and quickly accept the change we require. If we believe that God will use our heartache to teach us, to make our future better, and will bring us through and out of our heartache, and will make of us a better child of God than when we entered that heartache, we can endure. Hebrews 13:5 tells us, *"Let your conversation be without covetousness; and be content with such things as ye have...."*

"Caleb, it isn't easy to let go of the things we once cherished, but I am trying to accept that God allows devastating life changes to occur to help us learn and bring us into the fullness of His love and provision. This requires us to stifle our Adam-like nature and bring forth the new man, the Christ-like nature which God can bless and which He seeks for His new kingdom. It may not be easy for us, but once accomplished, will cause God to say of us: *"....Well done, thou good and faithful servant..."*. (Matthew 25:21)

Our strength lies in trusting that God is providing us with a new life through which we can become worthy and be ready when the bridegroom comes...and perhaps find a greater joy in what will be our new future! If we can endure our time of heartache and use it to learn and use God's words and thereby mature in our faith, we will be comforted. We can rest in the words of 1 Corinthians 15:58: *"Therefore, my beloved brethren, be ye stedfast, unmoveable...abounding in the work of the Lord....."*

But while Ann and Caleb spoke of these things with one another, they struggled inwardly with the hope that what they said and wanted to do would actually come to fruition.

Both still had their fears yet did not want to share them with one another....they wanted only to uplift one another. While they succeeded in word, both failed in deed to believe what they said to one another, thus both labored under guilt and felt unfulfilled when they parted. Caleb believed that he was doing what God wanted him to do for Ann and Ann felt that she was uplifting and comforting Caleb. Each harbored secret thoughts about wanting to retain the life they once had and both felt unworthy of God's help because of it. They did not understand that this was an abject failure in honest communication which contributed to their fears and brought guilt into their hearts. They felt that they were helping one another place their trust in God. Neither heeded Richard's warning that depression can impede one's healing both physically, mentally and spiritually. Thus Satan now had access to Ann and Caleb and could attack on many levels.

Caleb's surgery was a complete success and when he woke, he was relieved, but knew that he faced the challenge to walk again and to assist with his recovery. He was surprised to experience no pain upon awakening. His legs were encased in a multi-ribbed brace held fast by strips of Velcro. Its purpose was to prevent the knee from bending, so any movement at all had to be achieved with his legs straight. Later that evening two orderlies came into his room to get him out of bed for the first time. They raised the head of his bed so he was in a sitting position and helped him swing his legs toward the edge of the bed. Sitting up so suddenly made him feel dizzy and he had to rest in place for a moment before he could try to stand. As he slid his body closer toward the edge of the bed he laughed to see his encased legs sticking straight out from the bed, not bending thus preventing his feet from touching the floor. One of the orderlies placed a thick belt-like strap around his waist explaining that this would help them hold him securely. They explained how they would help him stand, one on each side as he reached for the handles on the walker which they had placed in front of him. Stiff-legged, working to get his feet under him, he stood…. and the pain washed over him with a vengeance. With both hands gripping the walker and an orderly on each side of him; one grasping the thick belt, he tried to take his first step. He'd been receiving pain medication every four hours, but still, the pain was severe. He took only a few steps and was returned to the bed, exhausted from the effort and the pain. The four days he remained in the hospital became a blur even though he was assisted in getting up several times each day to take a few steps. He wasn't used to lying on his back but the medication helped him sleep so it wasn't as unbearable as he'd thought it would be. He had no appetite and was surprised by how weak and lethargic he was. He was looking forward to traveling by ambulance from the hospital to the Rehab center where he would finally begin the work of walking again. The transfer from hospital bed to gurney and then from the gurney to the rehab bed was done so well that he was pleasantly surprised to experience no discomfort. Once he was made comfortable in the bed, he received instructions about how to call the nurse, how to turn on the television, and how to adjust the position of the bed. He was exhausted from the new instructions, the different activities and the anticipation, and promptly fell asleep. Ann arrived and was well pleased with the room and the facility and silently thanked Richard for his excellent choice. She found a coffee bar halfway down the hall and made two cups of coffee to bring back to Caleb's room. When she got back to the room Caleb was awake.

"Hi Honey", Caleb said, "Here's where I can begin to walk again!"

"Yes ….and you will feel better to be up and around…. and as you rebuild those muscles you'll be running again! But, I doubt that you can catch me yet!"

The nurses firmly instructed Caleb not to get out of bed by himself. They explained that he was to ring for a nurse and they would help him up and help him to the chair or to the bathroom. He was to use his walker or wheelchair at all times and was to have one or two people at his side when he got in or out of the bed or chair or bathroom…one of whom would hold his waist strap. He'd arrived at the Rehabilitation Center late on a Saturday afternoon and learned that there would be no physical therapy on Sunday. This gave him an entire day to become oriented to his new surroundings before beginning his therapy. When he needed to use the restroom, he rang for help as instructed and with help he sat up and scooted to the edge of the bed so he could swing his legs over the side of the bed in anticipation of standing and then, using the walker, make his way to the bathroom.

"Okay Celeb, on the count of three, me and Jim will help you up and then you can grab the handles of the walker to steady yourself. One, two, three!" Despite their help,

Caleb was surprised by how much he had to rely on his upper body strength to lift himself into a standing position. Sam, the orderly who was the most talkative, told Caleb that he was doing just fine. "Now, suh, if you all feel dizzy, it's natural…you been in bed for almost a week…so just give it a minute…just stand still for a minute before you try to take a step." Sam was right, he had felt dizzy, and nauseous, but in a minute or so he was fine and nodded to the orderlies that he was ready to go. Caleb was stunned by the pain. It was mostly in his calf muscles rather than in his knees and this made no sense to him. As he tried to take a step, his calf muscles contracted as if in a spasm. Because the pain was too great for him to walk, they had to place him into his wheelchair and wheel him into the bathroom. Once inside, Sam showed him how to grab the safety bar with both hands to pull himself into a standing position which had him facing the wall. Sam said that when he felt comfortable standing, he was to turn himself by taking baby steps just enough to ease himself to the high standing commode near his left hip. As he turned with one hand still on the safety bar and the other grasping the arm of the commode, he descended toward the seat. He felt the pain in his knees and as he sat. His legs, still encased in the stabilizers, came up into the air in front of him because the stabilizers prevented the knees from bending. He laughed to think of how silly he looked! Sam and Jim left the bathroom and stationed themselves outside the door after instructing Caleb to call them when he was ready to be transferred back to the wheelchair. In a few minutes Caleb began to question his ability to think. *Surely something has happened to my brain.....surely there is an answer to this dilemma and I'm just not thinking of it.* Caleb re-examined the high commode upon which he perched noting its high back support, its two high arms and the seat which was not deep enough to extend in front of his body. These conditions left him no access to his body. *Surely, I am not thinking correctly....surely there is a way around this situation...surely I am simply missing something here!* And so he sat...and thought. In time, Sam gingerly knocked on the door and asked Caleb if he was ready to return to his bed. Caleb, terribly embarrassed, told Sam that he seemed to have a lapse in memory for he could not figure out what he was to do to make himself ready! Sam stepped into the room and laughed as Caleb explained. "Haha, that's funny suh.....everybody says that one way or another....nope there ain't no way....them high commodes are just made that way. Someone who could invent one that was patient friendly could make a lot of money!"

"What" Caleb exclaimed. "There is no way for me to "care" for myself?"

"Suh, don't worry…we do this all the time!"

And Caleb had his first lesson in humility. He could not believe that someone had not designed a more customer friendly, independent supportive apparatus! Soon thereafter, and determined to find a way to handle his predicament, Caleb discovered that if he could pull himself up to a standing position by holding onto the grab bar, and balance himself upright he could then care for himself. Sam had also taught him how to use the recliner next to his bed which required a remote control to raise the seat of the chair to standing height. Caleb welcomed the idea that he could sit in the recliner to have dinner, or to watch TV or to simply be out of bed. Even though the chair's remote control brought the chair high off the ground so Caleb did not have to bend his knees to sit, it still hurt to bend that little amount to sit in the chair. Caleb involuntarily cried out despite his good intentions. But once he was seated the pain went immediately away and he was okay again. Sam helped position him and brought the call bell, water pitcher, telephone, and rolling dinner table within his reach.

"Take no mind suh of the pain, …it gets less as time goes on…..you'll get used to it and learn how to avoid it. Now, here's the call button and here's the table for your dinner tray. After dinner I can get you back into the bed."

Ann, hoping to have dinner with Caleb, had brought a sandwich and a bottle of cold juice for her dinner and pulled up the second chair in the room to sit across from Caleb. Her emotions tore at her heart. She was scared……and embarrassed to admit to anyone that she was scared. The family was so wonderful to her, taking care of the children, tidying the house, doing the children's laundry, even the food shopping. They spoke with such conviction that everything would be okay....that God was with them……so why couldn't she trust that way, why was she so terribly afraid? She felt unworthy, she felt that she'd let everyone down, especially God. And she didn't know how to fix what was wrong with her faith. So, once again she greeted Caleb with a smile and hid her fears and they enjoyed the evening together, both hiding their fears from one another.

That night Caleb could not sleep. He'd wake up every time he moved and attempt to turn to his side. He'd awaken from the pain of that effort and was thus forced to sleep on his back. *I will have to ask Richard how long it will take before I can sleep on my side.* Caleb was also instructed to plan when to ask for his pain meds so they would coincide not only with his physical therapy sessions, but also with his need to sleep at night. The next morning, before his first physical therapy session, Caleb had submitted to a shave and pretty much a body bath in bed, and then after breakfast, was taken via wheelchair by the physical therapist to the therapy rooms. Again he had to transfer from the bed to the wheelchair...no easy task. That however was to be a piece of cake compared to what he was to face for the next hour and then repeat again in the afternoon and again twice a day every day, for about three weeks or until he went home. The first thing the therapist did was assess how Caleb walked as he held onto the walker. But again Caleb's calves went into severe spasms. He forced himself to take two steps and then asked to sit down. He was wet with sweat. The therapist helped him into a chair and taught him how to use his arms to ease his body into and up from the seat. That first day he was taught how to do various types of leg lifts while sitting, then to squeeze a ball between his knees, then to slide his foot forward and backward using a strap under his arch to pull the leg back toward the underbelly of the chair thereby bending the knee. He also moved each leg from side to side. Each exercise was to be done thirty times alternating each leg at the count of ten. Before he was brought back to his room, his therapist tried to get him to walk again using the walker, but still his calf muscles cramped and the pain was too great. That afternoon, thinking he'd have to perform the same exercises once again, he was surprised to find himself on a cot, doing similar but slightly more difficult exercises while lying down. The therapist took a measurement of the angle in his bent knee to see what mobility he had for bending them. When the therapist pushed his shin while his knee was bent in an effort to get the best backward angle, Caleb again cried out in pain. The pain lasted only for a few seconds, so he decided that he could deal with it but came to dread that part of his therapy. Now he understood why the nurses always asked if he'd taken his pain meds before going to therapy! The pain medications had been ordered PRN meaning that the patient had to ask for them…they weren't simply given by rote. Because he had such difficulty walking, Caleb dutifully asked for the meds every four hours as instructed. A few days later he began to feel sick. He was dizzy, nauseous, weak, sweating, exhausted, sometimes shivering and depressed. It took another four days to discover that he was having an adverse reaction to the narcotic pain medication. He was still run down from the loss of blood, and from the trauma his body had been through and he therefore tired easily. This caused him to commiserate about how slow his progress seemed. He was still dependent on others for almost everything and he was shocked that he could not do what he had previously done in terms of his stamina. He was so sick that this put him back in terms of his therapy and made him despondent. He was also embarrassed to want to do something and be totally unable to do it. His mood went from frustration to anger....first with himself and then with the circumstances he had to face. He wanted to do additional exercises in his room but could not find the strength nor the incentive to do them. He finally succumbed to a lethargy which was hard to overcome. As Caleb sunk into a despondency which he hid from Ann he asked himself: *Will I ever be myself again? Why are my prayers unanswered.* His worries mounted once again. If he couldn't become functional by the time he left the rehab center, he was sure that he would be replaced at work. He convinced himself that his recovery could be advanced by putting more hard work into it. Yet his body was telling him something different and he had to accept the fact that his energy levels were low and his determination not as strong as he wanted it to be. He had to get his act together, he *had* to get better.

Caleb's mind worked overtime, dragging him down, then lifting him up and there seemed no answer to his dilemma until a visit from Matt and Jim brought an admission of his fears. Matt had been telling him what they were doing to help Ann and how everything at home was running "like clockwork" and therefore Caleb didn't need to worry about anything.

Caleb responded by telling them that his goal was to walk without cane or walker just so he could "pass the test" with his employer. If he could just "look" like he was back to normal, he could do the work. He knew that his men would help him and then, with just a little more time, he'd really be back and would make up for anything he'd been unable to do earlier. He decided that he would refuse to let his physical failures impact his life. He would make a success of this. He would! But then his voice broke and he admitted that the harder he tried, the slower he seemed to improve. His balance was off and he simply could not yet walk without the walker without endangering himself. He told them that he'd learned that because both knees were done at once, he'd have to re-educate the nerves which had been severed so his brain could send the right messages to his legs to help him with his balance. He also admitted that he did not understand why God allowed this into his life when he'd been trying so hard to be faithful, to learn, to teach, to be all that God asked of him. Matt and Jim were surprised to hear this from Caleb who'd always been their role model.....but now it was their turn to step up to the plate and do their part for Caleb.

"Caleb", Matt said, "I can't tell you how many times I've questioned God...it's natural.....the point is how we get back on track, not that we ever fell off! You are going through a lot right now, health worries, money worries, job worries, family worries....of course you'll question. But in the end the answer to your question will be that you will use your free will to decide to trust God and accept what He allows to come your way."

"I feel so guilty though Matt....I lay awake worrying even when I know inside that God is in control.... my mind won't stay calm, every past mistake, every current mistake, every possible future problem grows out of proportion and my inability to curtain it is almost killing me,"

"That's Satan. Pure and simple. And all you have to do is say aloud the word "NO" as soon as those thoughts begin...remember Grandma's advice? Then say aloubd some verse like "be not afraid" from scripture and those thoughts....at least in time.... will leave. Satan and his cohorts will eventually stop their attack. That's all it is....a spiritual attack and you know how to fight them."

"Gosh, how stupid I've been...I forgot about Grandma....and her sage advice to just yell "NO"! It always did work and I forgot about it. I guess I'll be spending some time tonight doing just that! But isn't it a sign of how weak my faith is?"

"No, it's just a sign that you are being tempted and a time when you will learn how to fight the temptation to give into those thoughts and allow them to dominate you. Everyone of us is tempted...attacked....at some time.....and it's a part of our learning process. It's how we come out of the battle that God watches, not how we might lose a skirmish or two."

Caleb was relieved by what Matt and Jim had said and how they responded to his....breakdown. He determined to do better. He was so grateful for his family, for their love, the their non-judgmental attitude and for their faith in him.

In truth, Caleb *was* progressing. It was just a very slow process. Every family member tried to encourage him by pointing out those things he could do today that he had not been able to do a week ago. He learned the value of therapists who would teach him what he could do on his own and he began to appreciate the incredible dedication of those who cared for him and worked so hard to help him. He memorized the names of every person who cared for him and soon developed a wonderful relationship with each one. He was delighted when they too wanted to speak about their faith. Soon he was doing much more for himself and happily singing in the shower finally feeling less embarrassed and more independent. But still, despite all this progress, Caleb could not help feeling that the healing process was far too slow and that he had to find a way to speed up his recovery. He was still feeling frustrated and impatient but now viewed those thoughts as natural. He still had to yell the word "NO" quite often, but he was making progress!

Chapter Eight

<u>TRUSTING AGAIN</u>

Four weeks after his surgery, Caleb could finally go home. For another four weeks, a physical therapist visited him at home three times each week and taught him how to perform the exercises which he would need to do for at least the next year. He was also taught how to walk with a cane rather than the walker and was finally given permission to drive. Therefore, eight weeks after Caleb's surgery, he went back to work for the first time. It was only part time…a few hours each day….but he was back!

He tired easily and felt a lot of pain if he sat for too long and then tried to stand. Once his legs got moving....maybe after six to eight steps, he could force himself to walk more properly...or so he thought. Nevertheless, being back at work also helped allay his worries about keeping his job. He did have to admit that though slow, he was improving, and that the more he walked and exercised his legs, the better off he was.

When Richard wrote the physician's order which allowed him to work, he'd made Caleb agree to visit an outpatient rehabilitation center three times a week. It was there that Caleb was put through a routine to coax the back of his legs to lie straight and flat against the workout table and to be sure that the knee would bend to a 130 degree angle or more. This was easier said than done. The exercises also improved his balance and helped him take longer, faster steps. When his muscles burned, when he began to sweat, when he had to push himself to bend and straighten his knees, he knew that he was doing what was required. He learned that it could take a year or even two years to be completely back to normal. He wasn't a happy camper to hear that news. But, he persevered and made progress. He was taught how to walk through an obstacle course where he'd step over bars of varied heights and balance on wobbly rounded plastic discs which looked somewhat like a flattened ball. He walked sideways wearing a thick rubber band around his ankles forcing him to use specific muscles. He also walked up and down the sample set of stairs at the gym and was surprised to find that coming down was more painful than going up. He used many of the machines specifically designed to increase muscle strength through resistance. But then.... there was the massage.

Initially Caleb had looked forward to this, as in his own mind, a massage was something relaxing and a great way to end the grueling exercises. However, Caleb was wrong. The massage was terribly painful...painful to the point of causing him to cry out and ask the therapist to stop. Its purpose was to locate small nodules of scar tissue or adhesions buried deep within the tissues. They were behind the knee, on the sides of the knee, up on the thigh and also on the scars themselves. Sometimes the therapists would attack them with their knuckles and this really hurt! "I *have* to break these up because they will limit your future mobility if they remain in place." they would say, "I'm sorry if I hurt you, but this *must* be done to allow you to regain your fullest mobility." Caleb would look at the clock on the wall and watch for the 7 to 10 minutes per leg to pass when the massage would be done. Then he'd have bags of ice on his knees for ten minutes and finally his torture was over for the day and he could soon hobble back to his car. He expected to find black and blue marks on his thighs as a result of the brutal assault on his flesh, but he never did. He almost wished he would find them so he could ask the therapist to let up a bit.

Sometimes he'd get despondent before going to the gym because he'd be thinking about the massage. Ann would chide him and ask, "Did you take your Advil Caleb? Did you pray, Caleb? Are you asking God to help you through the massage and the workout?" He did often forget to take the Advil but he did begin to pray more often and would sometimes wonder how many times each day he did pray.

He had once thought of prayer as those formal communications in the morning and at night and with each meal. But now he realized that many times each day he'd offer a quick sentence or two of thanksgiving, or one of intercession, or another of need. He found that he also informally talked to God about his life, his goals, his problems and his love for Him because he yearned for an intimate and personal relationship with his Heavenly Father. He wanted to say thank you and also to ask for help. He'd find himself feeling and expressing great emotion, especially when he spoke about his family and how God had always helped them. He understood that his prayers created a bond of faith and helped him share what lived in his heart. He also spoke of the pain of the heartache so many people in the world carried, or the difficult circumstance someone lived through, or how it felt to watch someone you love live through dire circumstances. He believed with all his heart that God could turn all heartache into a blessing by creating an opportunity to learn and to grow in faith from those circumstances. But he wondered how God felt when his children became emotionally exhausted as they lived through the pain of heartache. Caleb himself always felt guilty when he gave in to feelings of depression, or hurt, or emotional exhaustion because he feared that this indicated that he was not trusting God with the outcome. He tried to comfort himself by thinking: *God knows that emotional pain can be debilitating, as can our fears, and He knows that because we are impatient by nature, we long for the change and the lesson to be instantaneous. In time however, we learn that as we pray, and as we mature in faith, we increase our trust in God, and this in turn allows us to develop a peaceful heart no matter what our circumstances.* He'd think about prayer and how he desired to cover all the parts of a prayer he believed were important so he could offer a complete communication with his Heavenly Father. He remembered that Christ prayed for mankind and especially for those who would be faithful to Him and who would become what scripture termed, "The Bride of Christ". Loving these souls, Christ asked that His Father help them develop the faith they would need to be with Him forever.

Caleb recalled that the 17th chapter in John, (John 17:1-26) was devoted to the prayer Christ prayed for His followers and in John 17:25 Caleb had read: "...... *O righteous Father, the world hath not known thee: but I have known thee, and these have known that thou hast sent me.*"

It was through reading how Christ prayed that Caleb learned better ways to pray and how to touch the heart of God. He also remembered that scripture warned against repetitious and public prayers. Matthew 6:7 said: *"But when ye pray, use not vain repetitions as the heathen do......:* And when Caleb thought about what he should try to include in a prayer, he saw that all prayer should include praise, accountability, petition, protection, intercession and thanksgiving. Praise meant to acknowledge God for His goodness and power and mercy. Accountability required that one recount their sins, repent and ask for forgiveness. Petition was when we asked God for help in the matters which concern us. Protection was to acknowledge that God always helped us and that we should always ask for His continued protection. Intercession was when one prayed for those, alive and dead, in need spiritually and physically. Thanksgiving was to specifically thank God for all He has and will do for us. Caleb understood that a relationship with God meant that he truly communicate with Him and share the joys and sorrows in his heart. Repetition by rote did *not* encourage a close relationship, or provide a sincere heart to heart communication. By recounting his sins and the remorse he felt, he would be humbling himself before God; and he would be acknowledging his need for grace. Further, he tried to fill his mind with God's beautiful promises about prayer saying in Matthew 7:7: *"Ask and it shall be given you......"* But he also knew that this meant that God would give what was good for us if we bent our will to His.

Caleb had always taught his children to pray and to do so many times during the day. "Our morning prayer should include our thankfulness for what God has done for us and should contain a humble request for His guidance and protection throughout the day. Evening prayer should again contain our thankfulness for God's guidance and protection throughout the day, acknowledge His amazing love, grace and power, and be an intercession for others in need, and a humble request for Him to make us worthy. Before leaving the safety of our home, we should pray and ask God to accompany us and guide our steps, make our outing fruitful and secure through His protection. We should also pray before we eat to thank God for His provision and ask Him to remove the curse of the earth from the food and bless it for our use. Other prayers can be short and quick and cover an instant need or thank God for something special.

He remembered walking to the sliding glass window in their family room with the children and pointing out the birds circling the garden. He told the children what God said about them in Matthew 6:26. *"Behold the fowls of the air...they sow not, neither do they reap, nor gather into barns; yet your Heavenly Father feedeth them."* He'd also told them that if God took care of the birds, how much more would He care for His children and quoted from Matthew 10:29, 31: *""Are not two sparrows sold for a farthing? And one of them shall not fall on the ground without your Father....Fear ye not therefore..."*

Caleb taught his children that God does not want us to pray the same repetitious prayer over and over again because we rush through words so familiar that we don't hear or listen to their meaning. God wants us to have an *intimate* relationship with Him by talking with Him as we would with someone we love. Prayers that are short but from the heart are better than long memorized prayers. Neither does God want us to use our prayers publicly where we will be directing our attention to how we sound to an audience. Caleb explained that in Matthew 6:5, God warns, *"And when thou prayest.....be (not) as the hypocrites are: they love to pray...that they may be seen..."*

Caleb was grateful to those who prayed for him as he went through these changes in his life and remembered telling his children to intercede for others when they pray...even for those they have never met. He'd said, "We can ask our Heavenly Father to give a hearing unto all the pleas and petitions of His children all over the world. Then we can plead that if Our Heavenly Father cannot answer those prayers now, He will nevertheless, let His children know that He keeps them in the hollow of His hand; and offers them a peaceful heart. The power of prayer brings us the greatest rewards and can mean the difference between life and death, between hope and hopelessness, between foolishness and wisdom. James 1:5 says: *"If any of you lack wisdom, let him ask of God.....and it shall be given him."*

Caleb especially loved what he considered the most wonderful promise in scripture found in Deuteronomy 11:13-14: *".....if ye shall hearken diligently unto My commandments......to love the Lord your God and to serve Him with all your heart and with all your soul..... I will give you the rain of your land in his due season, the first rain and the latter rain, that thou mayest gather in thy corn, and thy wine, and thine oil."*

He'd said to his children, "Pray for wisdom in God's ways and ask for the wisdom to understand scripture and to place your steps where you will be pleasing in the sight of God. Little by little your understanding and your faith will increase and your thoughts and actions will follow accordingly. Praying with sincerity and to communicate with God brings about the changes we might require in our lives and results in a joyous peace and trust. Our prayers touch God's heart. He sees past our words and into our hearts. Nothing is hidden from Him. He knows whether or not we are truly humble, how thankful we are, and how sincere we are. He doesn't want us to pray by rote (Matthew 6:5-7) or to impress. He wants to hear a longing in us to be with Him, to serve him and those He loves. He wants to know that we *desire* to learn of Him and want to do our best to follow that which He asks of us. He wants to show us that He listens, He hears us, He loves us and has the power to change us, change our lives and create in us those who will be the Bride of Christ. That is the wonder of prayer!"

But after he spoke with the children and they were tucked into bed, Caleb pondered his words and felt like a hypocrite. He spoke the truth but did he follow that truth himself? Did he really trust God, Was he willing to give up everything for God? Hadn't he failed those tests by allowing his impatience and frustration and yes, even his anger, get the best of him? Could God still love him despite these failures? And what should he do about his attitude? When Ann joined him in the family room, he told her his concerns. She too admitted that she was worrying about how she had failed God for she couldn't seem to believe that everything would be okay in the end. She was still afraid. "What can we do Caleb? Will we be tested again and if so will we fail again? We are so strongly tied to what we have, what we have built over the years that I wonder if we are willing, *really* willing to give it up?"

"I don't know Ann, but I do know that I don't want to say no to God....I want to say 'yes', but somehow it seems so...final. To me it just seems that if we work hard, build a home, and provide for our children we should enjoy those fruits, and it just *doesn't* seem right to give it all up."

"Maybe God isn't asking us to give it up Caleb....maybe He just wants us to acknowledge our shortcomings, bring them to Him and trust Him enough to say...in spite of our fear....'Thy will be done'. Maybe He wants us humbled by our failure to live up to all we know we should, all He might ask of us. Maybe this is to help us appreciate the fact that *He* gave us everything we have and that we did *not* gain it because of our labor or talent or even because we deserved to attain it. Maybe our weaknesses and failures keep us humble and in need of God and the grace He offers us. Maybe it's more an attitude than an actuality when we have been born selfish and born sinners."

"How can we know this Ann? I don't want to fail God in *any* test of my love for Him yet this situation has indeed made me feel that I *have* failed. Maybe trusting Him fully is a process we have to grow into and by us living through this experience and, *by recognizing our shortcomings we can at least acknowledge them,* have remorse for them and ask forgiveness. But then again, we'd have to *want* to change, *strive* to change....and there again we may fall short. Maybe the first step, like you also said, is to recognize and acknowledge our shortcomings. And then see if we *really* have remorse for them, if we *really* wish we could overcome them.

Caleb, I feel the same, but I am also afraid. We have one another, we love one another, we have the children, a wonderful family, a church we love, ministers and fellow believers we love, we have been granted an understanding of God's plan for us, and still we fall short....still we are afraid to let go...afraid to *fully* trust. Why and what can we do to rectify this? How can we overcome our Adam-like sinful, demanding nature especially knowing that Satan will stalk us to the end of our days?"

"Satan wants to break our faith so he can pull us away from becoming one of God's chosen. Perhaps if we look deep inside ourselves, seek out our sins *and hate them*...we can ask for forgiveness and have that forgiveness granted."

"Oh Caleb, I hope so. You are right because there are so many who fail in other ways... and still God loves and forgives them. You know, like drug addicts, alcoholics who try so hard to overcome....and who *do* hate their condition and have remorse for it. God forgives them *if* they seek Holy Communion *worthily*. Maybe we must learn not to judge and to understand that every soul is a sinner and therefore no one person is really better than another....just on a different part of the path to the same goal. We have our failures, and others have theirs."

"Exactly Ann.....perhaps this shows us that we are not unique, we are all sinners, *all* have our failures and *all* of us must humble ourselves before God, acknowledging where we fall short, and must truly desire to be better than that, and ask for forgiveness. But what worries me is that Christ says that we should then, 'go and sin no more'!"

"Yes, that's worrisome Caleb because we continue to fall short. Though some people seem governed by evil. Some are so arrogant that they would never consider that what they do is wrong. Some have no concept of what it means to take Holy Communion *worthily*. But we must consider that there is the possibility that if we refuse to forgive someone and retain our judgment of them, it could be that God has answered *their* pleas for forgiveness and **they** will have **our** place at the wedding feast because of our refusal or inability to forgive. Perhaps what is imperative is that we overcome the tendency to make a blanket judgment about what others do. Scripture teaches us to love one another, care for one another, and forgive one another, but not to judge one another….that is up to God alone. Caleb, are we judging ourselves, perhaps? How does that fit in?"

"Hmmm….good question. Well, I think that we *have* to judge ourselves. We have to see the beam in our own eye before we look for any splinter in someone else's eye. I think that when we do look at ourselves….judge ourselves….and try to recognize what is lacking, we find it easier to understand someone else's plight. We can better understand that Satan holds someone hostage in one area just as he holds us hostage in another."

"Can we ever rest assured then Caleb that we are okay with God?"

"I am sure Ann that we can. Scripture tells us that we have to learn God's words by learning scripture....this way we know what He expects. Scripture teaches us about the sacraments or covenants which God offers us so we can come before His Holy presence. These are Holy Baptism which erases original sin, Holy Communion which forgives our sin and Holy Sealing which gives us the Holy Spirit so we can recognize even the subtlest of evils (Satan) and understand the truths of goodness (God)."

"Caleb, does everything we go through have a lesson in it? Was your accident planned by God to teach us something?"

"No Ann, God would never bring harm to His children. But Satan does and will. Because of God's righteousness and the war between Satan and God, God must allow Satan to tempt us, even hurt us. We have been given free will so we can ourselves choose between good and evil. God's righteousness doesn't allow Him to affect that choice. It has to come from us. But God, being omnipotent and omnipresent knows everything even before it happens. Much like the Fairy Godmother in the fairy tale titled "Sleeping Beauty" who tempered the effects which the evil witch planned for the heroin of the story. God tempers what Satan does to us and brings a blessing from it. Our job is to recognize what God wants us to learn from our experiences. Then it *has* worked for our good."

"All this can be so confusing yet so simple at the same time. It is truly a miracle of faith to be given this understanding of how Satan works and how God creates a blessing from the ashes of our sorrows. But why then do we still become so discouraged and fearful Caleb....why wouldn't we accept and be thankful...for everything?"

"Good question Ann.....it's probably because of our selfish self-centered nature which wants what it wants when it wants it, and probably because Satan constantly attacks our faith. I guess that our job is to understand this and hold tight to our trust in God no matter what the circumstances look like. Satan is a liar and tells us lies about ourselves and about how God could never love us when we fail."

I feel better now Caleb, thanks! But, we'd better get to bed now...we have a busy and early day tomorrow."

"Ann, remind me often of these words so that I don't give in so easily to negative thoughts and that I thank God for these circumstances and where they will bring us."

"Okay Caleb, but only if you will do the same for me!"

Chapter Nine

AMAZING GRACE

Caleb was angry; mostly with himself. But anger always finds a way to affect everyone who might be around the person expressing that anger! Caleb's main complaint was that he still wasn't walking correctly after three long months of struggle.... and he wanted some answers. What was wrong? Was it something *he* wasn't doing? Was something wrong with the implants? Was it some failure of his body? He was faithfully walking on the treadmill at the gym and seemed to walk perfectly well on that. He was walking for a half hour after each session unrelated to whatever walking he did at home or on the job. Yet, when he tried to walk as fast and as steadily as he did on the treadmill, he found himself wobbly, waddling in fact, and afraid that he might fall. His patience was sorely tried. Why were some sections of the incisions at the top of his knees not responding to the scar-diminishing medication Richard had recommended. He'd diligently applied the salve as instructed and watched the miracle take place on most of the scarred area but not on all. Why?

When he mentioned his concerns about walking correctly to the therapist, he was told that a treadmill does not accurately mimic regular walking; that it in fact eliminated the natural push-off process of the feet. Holding the handles of a treadmill was similar to using a walker which eliminates the need to use the legs, feet, and toes for balance. "Then what you are telling me", Caleb replied, "is that I need to practice, day in and day out to walk, *without* cane, *without* walker, *without* treadmill if I want to regain my balance and walk correctly?"

"Yes. And you also need to walk a little faster and take longer steps. You need to concentrate on *lifting* your legs as you put them forward to eliminate the "waddle" as you describe it. You are supposed to not only lift your leg at the *knee* but also at the *hip* to create the perfect step. What we can do here is place the holding belt around your waist and walk with you so you become accustomed to the faster pace and longer step to reduce your fear of falling. We can also assess how you raise your legs when you walk inside the safety bars over an obstacle course....and we can have you stand on one leg inside the safety bars without holding onto to the rail and hold that position for thirty seconds and then switch legs."

"Why didn't you tell me this earlier?"

"Caleb, each part of the rehab is planned so you can progress systematically, so we will be addressing all these issues, but you have to admit that you put a brave face on everything and don't let us know what your concerns. With each evaluation we increase weights, up the level of the exercises, determine how far we can push you......but we can't see what you do when you leave here....unless you tell us. If you don't let us know what's wrong, even when we ask, we can't make those additional corrections......you have to *communicate* with us and *help* us help you. Now that we understand that you feel that you are not walking the way you should, we will make an assessment and work on it more thoroughly. I think that you will find that it's not anything other than you not practicing how to walk *properly*. You have all the tools, you have the strength, and you have healed enough, so you just have to do it…. and we will help you!"

Caleb, watching himself in the mirror saw that he was swinging his right leg around to walk rather than lifting the foot by bending it at the knee and hip and moving it forward. When he concentrated on what he was doing wrong, he could walk correctly after all. "So this is why the front of my shoe sometimes grabs the floor!!" The therapist told him that more than likely, he'd been walking this way for years and doing it unconsciously. Once he understood what he was doing wrong, he concentrated on the lift and was determined to eliminate the compensating swing of his leg. He was so pleased with himself and at the same time so angry not to have understood what he was doing wrong a lot earlier. His therapist explained that even if he had noted this earlier he might not have been strong enough at that point to make the correction.

To eliminate the need for Caleb to change clothes when he left work to go to the gym, Ann had slit the outside seam of two pair of his slacks from the knees down and added

Velcro to the seams. While at work, and behind the desk and even during his therapy he could open the Velcro to let the clothing fall away from his scars. And, in therapy he could open them for the flat exercises and for the massage. The therapist could therefore assess Caleb's scars and the remaining marks from the 35 staples in each knee which had been removed ten days after his surgery. The two scars were still red and ugly and caused discomfort when a blanket or clothing touched them. Caleb asked if it was true that the scar-diminishing salve would not work on any scar which had been in the sun for any length of time. He was concerned because while in the Rehab center he'd sometimes sat outside in the wheelchair with his knees exposed to the sun. "Why wasn't I told?" he asked. "I could have avoided the sun!"

His therapist told him to keep using the salve and to rub it gently into the scarred area to break up any adhesions. He felt that in time and despite the exposure to the sun, the scars would diminish. "There is so much to know about this surgery and rehabilitation process that most patients would be overwhelmed by so much information. Therefore we try to explain as we go along and to help where we can, but it is just so much to know and on top of that every patient is different…each one has a different healing time, a different pain threshold, a different need to understand, and even a different degree of exercise to which they will respond." This made sense to Caleb but he was glad that he'd asked his questions and received the answers.

When he'd made his first post-op visit to Richard's office, an xray of his new knees found them perfect. Caleb still had questions. He wanted to know whether or not his new knees would set off the metal detectors when entering a government facility or an airport. He was disappointed to learn that he would surely set off the alarms because the newer sensitive detectors would be alerted despite his new knees being made from titanium. Caleb also wanted to know why his knees felt so heavy. Richard smiled at Caleb's questions and, understanding his level of curiosity explained, "Ya know Caleb, one leg alone is about one quarter of your total body weight and the new knee only weighs 8 or 9 ounces, so it isn't its weight you feel, it's just the swelling you feel, and the numbness and weakness... and the muscles, tendons and ligaments readjusting which make your legs feel heavy and stiff.... and all that will disappear in about one year."

"Ahh Richard, there is so much for a patient to learn....shouldn't there be a check list for patients?"

"It would be too confusing Caleb because there are so many aspects to this type of reconstruction. It would however, be a good idea for each subject to have its own checklist for whenever a specific question arises."

"Yeah…and who would create this information, and where would this be stored, and how would the patient know that it's available? Logistics…I know…logistics!"

But even with all this new information and all the progress he was making, Caleb was frustrated. He wanted to get back to his old self…. now…..not in one year…or two! Sometimes his frustration over how slow his recovery was caused him to lose his temper. He understood that everyone, good or bad, gets angry. God even gets angry. Christ too, once became so angry that He overturned the market tables inside the gates of the temple. He knew however, that there are differences between feeling anger, expressing anger, and maintaining anger. He understood that anger is a natural consequence of the Adam-like nature and as we move from the Adam-like nature to the Christ-like nature we learn…and desire… to control our anger.

Initially, he thought, *we feel anger, but feeling anger can move into expressing anger which comes in two forms; one* is productive and the other negative. Productive expression is when we calmly acknowledge, and explain why we felt anger over a certain situation, and what we believe should be put into place to prevent the cause of that anger in the future. This helps us avoid circumstances which cause anger and helps us communicate our feelings and needs to those with whom we interact.

Negative expression occurs when we openly express our feelings in a manner which angers others and we offer no constructive explanation of, or methods for, preventing the cause of our feeling or expression. A negative reaction demonstrates that we have not controlled our anger, have not directed it toward solutions based in love and respect, and that we do not actively seek resolution. This is detrimental to those around us and detrimental to our soul salvation.

The act of maintaining our anger is encouraged by Satan and must be overcome. The memory of what caused our anger may serve to keep us from harm, but the maintenance or harboring of anger works to cloud our judgment, prevent change and growth, and robs us of love. It also robs us of the ability to maintain the fruits of the Holy Spirit which strives to guide us toward the godly love *expressed by Christ. Harboring anger can also make us ill because it destroys our peace and creates anxiety, hate, and other detrimental emotions. It also means that we have not forgiven.*

Caleb also knew that scripture explained that in time the power of love and prayer, and of our personal example, can create a message which can take root in others. Psalm 133:1 says, *"Behold, how good and how pleasant it is for brethren to dwell together in unity!* Therefore since we provide a subtle message through our personal behavior, it carries a far stronger impact than we think. He knew that he was angry with himself and that being angry can itself cause suffering not only to him but to everyone around him. He also knew that God offers us a blessing for handling our anger correctly. *We receive something incredibly valuable by handling our anger correctly. Satan may inspire the anger, but God can turn it into a blessing for us. This is one of the most magnificent miracles of our life of faith: that what can harm us can be turned into something which can help us if we know how God wants us to handle it. God works in mysterious ways and if we learn how this process works, we can overcome a great deal. We can help ourselves and we can help others. We can stand firm when we work to subdue our anger knowing that God loves us and will create a miracle from our experience. Even if we fall prey to fear or anger temporarily, we can work out of it, rise above it and bring joy to the heart of God in the process.*

He remembered that Colossians 3:21 tells us: *"Fathers, provoke not your children to anger, lest they be discouraged."* That Hebrews 13:16 tells us: *"..... do good ......for with such....God is well pleased."* That Matthew 7:12 says: *".....whatsoever ye would that men should do to you, do ye even so to them...."* That Proverbs 16:24 tells us: *"Pleasant words are as a honeycomb; sweet to the soul, and health to the bones."* And that Proverbs 8:32 tells us: *"....for blessed are they that keep my ways."*

Anger has its place and sometimes we must be angry. But in most cases we become angry over something that doesn't really matter and scripture teaches us that the bottom line is to flee from evil, love the soul, and keep peace with one another. Work together to learn and teach God's words to be a part of the First Resurrection, and overcome the traps Satan lays for us.

Our job is to continually examine with honesty if we are doing what God asks of us. We are to let our anger go and *to forgive all harm even if we must remember that harm to protect ourselves in the future. We are **not** asked to remain in the company of those who enjoy hurting others. So why should anyone remain in my company when I am always so angry and frustrated?* "For God shall bring every work into judgment, with every secret thing whether it be good, or whether it be evil." Ecclesiastes 12:14

So Caleb, knowing that he was often terse with Ann and the children, especially when he was in pain, decided to try to curb his anger and to make life more pleasant for those around him. He was making progress. He could get up from most chairs now without terrible pain, he could sit with knees bent for longer periods of time, and......he was walking now without any support whatsoever. Richard had warned him right up front that it could take a year maybe two years for him to heal, and for him to feel that his knees are a part of him; "normal" again. Therefore, he'd just have to accept his situation and recognize that he needed forgiveness for how ungrateful he was and how he took his frustrations out on everyone around him. He realized too that Ann had been his "gofer" for months now....bringing him coffee, picking up a magazine that he couldn't easily reach, driving him everywhere until he could drive himself. He realized that having both knees done at one time created the need for a longer rehabilitation period, and that Ann had never complained. He could not help her, but she helped him with everything during this time. He owed her a great deal and what had he given her but complaints.

He remembered when he'd gotten a head cold about three months into his recovery and she'd run out to the store to get cough syrup and lozenges, and had made many pots of chicken soup. Had he thanked her? Had he appreciated all she'd done? Had he taken her for granted? In fact, even Joe and Preacher had done a lot for him. They'd visited the hospital and at the rehab center, they visited even when he was at home again. They climbed ladders to change the light bulbs which had gone out on the vaulted ceilings of the family room. They kept him up to date with what was happening at work......and.....they covered for him at work. Not that he'd needed any covering, but he could see how they always made a point of giving him credit for the work they'd done whenever the big bosses were in. Had he shown them any appreciation?

Caleb suddenly thought about how remiss he'd been and what he needed to do to make amends. He realized that one of the most difficult things a truly loving Christian is required to learn is how to say "I'm sorry". And then to forgive themselves. He also knew a lot of men who could easily forgive others, but the mistakes they'd made either before they became a Christian or as they were growing in faith often came back to their thoughts and caused sleepless nights and anguish. Retracting past actions and words is not possible and can therefore be replayed in our minds over and over again with us wishing that those circumstances had not occurred. He thought about how securing the forgiveness of those we hurt helps toward resolving how often the mind replays our mistakes. Making restitution also adds to the resolution of the concerns we experience. But often, the person we hurt may have died, may have relocated, might have refused to provide forgiveness, or would use the opportunity to bring harm again. This precludes the closure so helpful in resolving guilt and forgiving ourselves. However, there is another element to this dilemma which Christians should consider and that is how pride can hold someone back from apologizing or admitting an error. Caleb realized too that he was a perfectionist and often expected a high standard of both behavior and work ethic from others. *Many of us are perfectionists. We work hard, do our best, and push ourselves to perform at a high level of achievement. This can be a very good trait. However, sometimes the gifts we have been given which allow us to perform at this level become mixed with pride. We are proud of our achievements and proud of the hard work we willingly placed into those achievements. But pride has no place in our Christian life.*

He remembered that God said in Proverbs 29:23, "*A man's pride shall bring him low....*" He knew that pride comes from Satan and can easily cause us to put so much of ourselves into our achievements that we no longer take time for God. We can also begin to believe that it is our own efforts which created the achievement rather than God's blessing. Loving the achievement excessively can be devastating if it is taken from us. *Maybe that's what's holding me back*, he thought.

When we have great pride we also begin to view ourselves as exceptional and want others to do the same. Thus when we are forced to admit that we have not been perfect in the eyes of God, our pride is hurt and subconsciously this creates the need to feel good again about ourselves. This need causes us to enter into a never ending cycle of thoughts which are made up of fear, guilt and concern over our personal failures. Rather than keep us humble they make us angry at the situation which *forced* us to become imperfect. Satan wants these emotions to create a barrier to the love, protection and forgiveness of our Heavenly Father. But once we know to watch for pride, to acknowledge that all we have comes from God and not through our own achievement, we can overcome. We can free ourselves of the pride, anger and guilt which creates the inability to forgive ourselves. Thus there can be a multitude of lessons in our struggles and we can be thankful that God so patiently brings us into an awareness of those things which we need to address so we can grow into the bride He wants for His Son. We can also see how a blessing is created from our heartaches. Caleb had no idea that Ann had already become aware of the danger of pride and now the Holy Spirit opened it up to Caleb as well. Caleb then decided to do his utmost to let everyone know how much he appreciated their help and how sorry he was to have let his anger and pride cause him to hold back the love and thanks he should have been giving them. He thought about the song "Amazing Grace" and thanked God for opening his understanding to these faults and helping him recognize the grace he'd been given, not only by God, but also by the family and friends who were so faithful to him. He was the luckiest man in the world.....no....the most blessed and he wanted to make things right!

While Ann and Caleb were learning what God wanted to teach them, so too were Joe and Preacher, Richard and Rachel, Matt and Sarah, Jim and Barbara, Josh and Deb, Mary and Kevin, Elizabeth and Rebecca, Ruth and Wade, Jayden, and all their children learning. They had been listening to Ann and Caleb and watching and understood the magnitude of what had occurred.... financially, physically and spiritually. Each thought about what they would do if they were in Caleb's shoes. Each saw the struggles, the fears...and then the strength of faith and the answers that Ann and Caleb took from those experiences. And each understood that something similar could happen to them.....and they needed to pray, to learn, to prepare for a spiritual attack...and be ready to come through such a circumstance. And even Joe's heart was touched. The example that this family showed him......not their temporary worries...but the end result of their faith and how they pulled together had really impressed him. He wanted to learn more about how they obtained such a faith and become what they were. Unbeknownst to each of them, they became Joe's role models, and maybe....just maybe he would admit this one day to Preacher.

Chapter Ten

TRUE HEALING

Caleb asked Ann if they could plan to have a fellowship at their home. He wanted to invite the entire family, and to include Richard and Rachel and also many people from work. Ann was delighted by the prospect. When she phoned Sarah and Barbara, Mary and Elizabeth, Debbie, Ruth and Rachel they all talked her into allowing them to each bring something to eat. Just as they had been bringing wonderful dishes to Ann's house, they planned to coordinate what they would bring to the party so that an entire meal could be created, from the nibbles to the entrée to the dessert! Ann was so thankful for their love and support and sent a prayer for them to God. It seemed that everyone was thrilled to attend the fellowship and on that day the house overflowed with people, all talking at once. The aroma of some very wonderful recipes floated from the open kitchen causing mouths to water. It was a beautiful fall day and the French doors were opened to the roofed patio past which the flowers bloomed in profusion and in joyous celebration of the gathering. Ann smiled, thinking that once again they were back where they loved to be....with family and friends. She could hear Preacher's loud voice again proclaiming his faith to Joe by saying: "We know that Christ died for our sins and that His death was the perfect sacrifice through which our sins can not only be forgiven but wiped from all record spiritually. If scripture teaches us these truths and if we believe what scripture tells us, then from where does our continued anguish originate? It surely cannot come from God but does come from Satan. Satan's job is to destroy our faith. He believes that by doing this he can prolong his freedom. To destroy a Christian's faith requires a personal attack on his hope, his courage, and his ability to trust. If Satan can successfully attack a Christian on these fronts, he may break an otherwise strong faith. If he can cause us to be depressed, filled with guilt, tired and exhausted from our thoughts of the past and fear of the future, he can wear us down. We need, then to ask ourselves why Satan would have this power over us and what we need to do to thwart this type of spiritual attack."

Ann's attention moved away from Preacher and toward Debbie who was talking about the plight of young people today. "Sadly, many young people dwell on the hurt caused by a broken relationship. This not only exacerbates their emotional and physical pain, but it also brings them a great deal of guilt, anger and distrust which compounds their pain. They must move on, but must also examine the underlying causes for the broken relationship. To avoid a repeat of the situation which could bring that same harm to them again in the future, they must begin to understand and recognize the selfish nature, the ungodly nature, and the indiscriminate nature in self and others so they can learn how to build better future relationships. If one feels that they have been a part of the problem, they must do as much for themselves as they do for others by forgiving themselves, by not carrying guilt, but by doing better in the future by remembering the lesson. One must bring the problem to God and then trust Him to help. To make the pain of a perceived loss subside one must forgive the soul and forget the incident but carefully consider and remember what to avoid in the future. God wants us to forgive, but has not asked us to forget what should become a protective measure or learning experience. He may have allowed a broken relationship to make us a better and wiser person in the future, or to protect us from a relationship which would not have fostered the growth of our spiritual life."

Ann looked over toward Matt and Josh, marveling that everyone seemed to be talking in some way and through many subjects about their faith. Matt was saying: "The end time is a dangerous era for all Christians. It is a time of great power for Satan and if we are not spiritually prepared, his anger and desperation can bring us serious harm not only spiritually, but also emotionally and physically. Thus we must remember just as we must forgive. We must be watchful and discerning just as we are giving and kind. We must not let our guard down as these end times envelop us and we must remember that God clearly warns in Mark 13:20, "....except that the Lord hath shortened those days, no flesh should be saved....." We each have a responsibility to be prudent, and to be aware of evil, and to 'watch'. 1 Peter 4:7 tells us, *"But the end of all things is at hand.....watch....."* 1 Peter 5:8 says, *".....your adversary the devil......walketh about, seeking who he may devour."* We cannot watch nor be vigilant if we forget our lessons or if we never grow from them."

As much as Ann appreciated their faith, it was time for them to just have fun and to rejoice that they were all together again after so many weeks of hospital visits. Earlier, she'd contacted Rebecca and Jayden to ask them if they'd help her get everyone involved in playing a game. They'd agreed to help and planned to initiate the game right after everyone had eaten. For now, with the barbeque fires going and the bowls of food being laid out on the long serving table, it was time to pray for the food and get to the business of watching it disappear!

Since Jim had recently become a deacon in their church, they asked him to pray for the blessing on the food. They all marveled when Jim prayed remembering how he'd resisted God when he'd first married Barbara and had been so sarcastic when any of them spoke about their faith. But God had worked a miracle in Jim's heart and shown him that He did indeed exist and did indeed have a good reason for everything that happened in the world.

Jim asked God to bless their gathering, bless everyone who had so graciously contributed the food and to bless the home where the fellowship was held. He also asked that Caleb be healed and that they all would be found worthy. It was a joy not only to hear the adults say "Amen" at the end of the prayer, but also to hear the tiny sweet voices of the children, even the littlest ones just beginning to talk to chime in with their loud "Amen's".

Then everyone began to fill their plates and enjoy the food. They drifted to all the areas where they could sit to eat: from hearth, to table, from couch and cocktail table to open patio, and again the conversations began to flow. Altogether, there were 22 adults and 17 children in attendance and because of the open floor plan Caleb and Ann had so meticulously designed for such fellowships, everyone had a place to sit where they could still see and even hear one another as needed. Ann's heart swelled with thanksgiving.

When dessert was served, Caleb told everyone that he had an announcement to make and silence fell on the group. Caleb began by thanking them all for coming, reminding them that each of them had a very special place in his heart. "I want to say that I'm sorry for all the times that I may have let my frustrations and anger affect you....I know I was a bear......but still you were all there for me...for Ann...over many months...as we struggled to get through this accident. I want to thank you for your prayers because without them I would never have found peace. Christ provides one of the most wonderful offers to counteract our lack of peace in John 14:27 where He says, *"Peace I leave with you, my peace I give unto you: not as the world giveth, give I unto you. Let not your heart be troubled, neither let it be afraid."*

"This is very powerful. What these words tell us is that when we pray, we can thank God for the peace He has provided for us, but also remind Him that Christ promised that we could also have His peace. We can ask for this in our prayers and ask that it work to still our troubled heart and mind. If this approach is not sufficient, then we need to be introspective and take a good look at ourselves so we can search for what might be holding us back from finding that peace. If we have asked for forgiveness from God, if we are truly remorseful, if we are striving to never commit that act again, and if we have partaken of Holy Communion... and still have no peace, then we must look inward. Satan has looked into our heart and found something which he is using to his advantage. 2 Corinthians 2:11 warns: *"Lest Satan get an advantage"*.

"Well, on many occasions Satan did get the advantage over me and I was terribly discouraged and could not find peace. But because of your love and your prayers and your incredible support...we've come through everything..... and I just wanted you to know how very much we appreciate all you have done. Thank you...you have all been such a blessing to us!"

"Hear, hear" Preacher shouted...."You are forgiven Caleb even though you *were* sometimes a grump! So there....so now ....just *fuh-ged-a-boud-it*! And we all thank you and Ann for this great fellowship and good food! And, ya know what...we thank you for how you stuck it out and remained faithful through it all."

Everyone joined in agreement, laughing at how Preacher spoke of Caleb's occasional frustration and in full agreement that the end result was so favorable, physically and spiritually. Soon the chattering began again. Rebecca and Jayden gathered up the plates and utensils and Elizabeth began to pack up the leftovers so they could be refrigerated. Barbara put out a few bowls of pretzels, bowls of individually wrapped chocolates, a platter of baby carrots, small celery sticks for the diet conscious, and some bowls of mixed nuts so there was still plenty to nibble on.

"Okay everyone. We are going to play a game", Jayden announced. "The children can play too."

"We will split into teams of men against the women, each team taking one question. If that team cannot answer or gives a wrong answer, the opposing team gets a shot at it. Andrew is going to keep score...with me helping. Rebecca and Heza will take turns asking the questions. Okay? Here's the first question....and Ladies first! Rebecca?"

"Here's an easy question: Who are we? I really liked my mother-in-law and she gave me some hints about catching a new husband when her son died.

The men joked about this question being a new take on the old mother-in-law jokes while the women conversed about the answers they would give. But then Preacher yelled out: "Ruth". He was beaming with joy because he knew the answer.

"No, no, no Preacher....that was a question for the women and now you've gone and given them one of the answers!"

"Oh my gosh, yes" he said, "I'm sorry".

"We'll just start over with a new question" Rebecca said.

But then Joe piped in and said, "You know, the relationship that Ruth had with her mother-in-law Naomi is very much like what I see between all of you."

"How's that Joe", Preacher asked.

"Well, all the conversations we've had...*you've* all had...from the moment that Caleb had his accident.....well even sooner actually......has really taught me something. I used to resent Preacher's constant lecturing about his faith and now I look forward to it. I've watched all of you and seen that you are really no different from me in terms of your worries and concerns, your strengths and your weaknesses......but.......the difference is that as soon as you talk about the situation you all seem to dig down deep somewhere and conjure up that free will that you are always talking about. Like Ruth and Naomi you have a commitment to one another which helps you help one another actually apply your free will to *choose*...to *decide*....to *will* yourselves to trust God with your circumstance. You understand that each of you at some time or another struggle to do this, but it is what you all finally do. That's actually what brings you through that problem. I used to think that I was so much more a failure and just kinda gave up on faith and God and stuff......but you taught me that we are *all* failures unless we make that kind of decision, *use* that free will to trust...to turn it over to God. So, I just want to say 'thank you' for letting me be a part of all this and a special thanks to Preacher for not giving up on me."

"Gosh Joe, I'm....I'm.....well...I don't know what to say, except how happy I am."

"Aw Preacher, now don't go getting all teary eyed, I'm still gonna beat you down when you lecture too much....but I can see now that it's just...well...when you love your faith so much...it just has to overflow to others....you just *have* to share it."

"Yeah, yeah, that's it Joe." Preacher replied.

"Well, for me", said little Andrew..."I know I'm just a little kid and I know that you think I'm just playing my games while you're all talking but I hear things too....and I worry too.....and at first I even cried...although I never told anyone. But then, listening to Mom and Dad kinda talk it out and do what Uncle Joe said...ya know.....talk about how

God helps us...and what He promises us...'n stuff.....I felt better. And ya know, I could pray better after listening to Mom and Dad talk because I sorta knew then what we are supposed to do. So, this helped me learn too."

Ann and Caleb had tears in their eyes, so grateful were they that their conversations had always moved toward what God wanted them to do and had therefore been good for Andrew.

Sarah, to lighten the moment said, "Andrew we are all so proud of you and because you have learned so much you will be the role model for all the children....so whenever anyone has a problem, you will know how to help!"

"Yes Aunt Sarah, I can do that."

"Well let me tell you what I've learned", Jim added. "As you all know, I came late into this faith and came kicking and screaming that God did not hear our prayers and was wrong to allow so much heartache in the world. I finally began to understand the process of development. What I saw here was another lesson about development. If we are honest with ourselves and not caught up in pretending to be holy rollers all the time, we can share our fears and misgivings, our failures and our grief. We can talk about these things too because as we do, something happens inside us...probably the prompting of the Holy Spirit.....to teach us that we all feel these things from time to time and that our job is to overcome them simply through trusting God. And that occurs just as Joe said by us *deciding* to trust. As soon as we do that something magical happens and we find peace. I think it's that Satan leaves and we no longer suffer from his attack. Yeah, he comes back to try again, but the more often we make that conscious decision, the stronger we become and the quicker we get through the next attack."

Caleb added, "It's not easy to admit to our imperfections, but how can we learn if we don't...in fact acknowledging our sins is an important part of being forgiven. Ann and I held back from admitting our fears to one another, but when we finally did we felt better and we could work on fixing what was wrong. Everyone hates to admit to their weaknesses, but when we do we overcome pride.....and when we do not judge one another for those weakness we develop a trust in one another that really cements a relationship."

The game forgotten, everyone began chattering about what a great exchange they'd had and how it impacted their own take on why bad things happen to good people...it was a growth process which the true children of God should welcome and seek out the lesson in it.

Once again they'd all had a great fellowship. The women had everything cleaned up and put away in no time, the men carried the trash out to the containers in the garage, and moved the furniture back to their correct places. Even the chair legs were matched to the slight indentations they'd left in the Oriental carpet upon which they originally stood.

Caleb asked John to pray for everyone's safe journey home. John thanked God for their fellowship, for love one another and asked God to bless Ann and Caleb for opening their home to everyone and to help Caleb to a full recovery. He thanked God for allowing them to learn yet another lesson for their development. When the door closed on the final guest, and Andrew and Lorraine had voluntarily gotten into their respective beds exhausted from the festivities, Ann and Caleb felt that this was a new beginning for them.

But Satan doesn't give up easily. He wanted another shot at breaking Caleb and Ann's faith. He had one more ploy up his sleeve which he was sure would work to bring this family down.

Chapter Eleven

REACHING OUT

Both Ann and Caleb understood that everyone makes mistakes, that Satan uses people to harm people. They knew that some of these people are good people who fall prey to the mistakes Satan inspires in them while others are not concerned about what God wants of them. Both Caleb and Ann had been taught to remember this, and to work to weed out what they allowed to live in their own heart. They tried to discern what lives in the heart of others to avoid certain situations in the future while taking care not to judge in this process. They knew that evil circles and tempts everyone and therefore they must remember the lessons attached to their mistakes as well as those attached to the mistakes of others. These must act as a warning not to be tempted to engage those situations again. They understood that if their relationships are with souls who do *not* seek God, and scoff at those teachings, they might become unequally yoked whereby one or both who share that yoke will inevitably fall. They also knew that when Scripture teaches that we are to arm ourselves with the word of God it does so to help us become aware of the spiritual wickedness which seeks to devour us. The armour which scripture speaks of is God's words and His instruction. These and the might of God become our protection. When our heart is right with God and we fully understand what He asks of us, what dangers we face, and what our future will be, and we strive to please Him, we will always have His guidance and protection. When we have gained the wisdom, courage and self-esteem to learn and overcome, to have fellowship with others willing to do the same, and to teach those who do not yet understand, we have matured enough to have something of value to offer. But if we remain complacent in godly matters, and desperate in personal matters, and live without introspection we cannot grow spiritually and may make the same painful mistakes over and over again. When we lose trust in God when encountering our difficulties, we have not developed a relationship with Him nor learned that we *can* trust Him.

Caleb and Ann understood that one of the many precious gifts God provided for them is the promise that if they sincerely *strive* to learn and do what He asks, He will reward them immensely. They'd always marveled at the words in Matthew 25:21 which said: *".....thou hast been faithful over a few things, I will make thee ruler over many things......."* They knew that God referred to them as His children and that He expected an expanding maturity to occur in them so they could grow into the bride of Christ. 1 Corinthians 13:11 explained: *"When I was a child, I spake as a child, I understood as a child, I thought as a child, but when I became a man, I put away childish things."*

It wasn't easy to overcome their selfish nature but if they did the reward would be great for Revelation 2:11 promised: *"....He that overcometh shall not be hurt in the second death."* And verse 26: *"And he that overcometh and keepeth my works unto the end, to him will I give power over the nations."*

One evening, as Ann and Caleb sat near the fire, they asked Lorraine and Andrew if they wanted to join in a discussion about what God hoped we would become. Andrew and Lorraine were delighted feeling that they were now really "adults".

"Caleb", Ann began, "I understand that perfection cannot be attained while we are in the flesh and living in Satan's territory and that God rewards our striving to apply His words to our lives. He wants us to be contrite when we fail and be thankful for the forgiveness of sin. These help us lay aside our former failures and create an overcomer in God's eyes. But what happens when we keep on making the same mistakes over and over again?"

"Well" Caleb answered, "Scripture does say....in Romans 12:2, *"Be not conformed to this world; but be ye transformed by the renewing of your mind, that ye may prove what is that good and acceptable and perfect will of God."* And Galatians 5:1 warns, *"Be ye not entangled again with the yoke of bondage."* This tells us that we can become entangled again even after we break away from sin and even after God himself frees us. Thus, to be an overcomer, we need to protect ourselves from the traps which might once again engage us, and even in this God provides us with how we can reach our goal. The armour of God is mentioned often throughout scripture and tells us that God, aware of our fragility, offers us protection. Ephesians 6:11 says, *"Put on the whole armour of God, that ye may be able to stand against the wiles of the devil."* This tells us that without the armour God provides we may not be able to stand against evil. Romans 13:12 teaches, *".....cast off the works of darkness and..... put on the armour of light."* And....there is not much time left before Christ returns. When He does return, it will be too late to change."

"Daddy," Andrew added, "In Sunday school were learned that the armour God's gives us is called righteousness and righteousness is our faith....and....and that faith comes from our relationship with God."

"Yes," Lorraine said, "I learned that too, and that we have to have to learn what God wants, work hard to do it and always take Holy Communion to be forgiven when we make a mistake."

"That's right...my, little darlings, I am so proud of you!" Ann replied, "Perhaps you have also learned that the word "darkness" is refers to what is evil and the word "light" represents Christ and all He taught and all He sacrificed for us. So, if we want to obtain the armour or protection of God, we must denounce all things which are the works of darkness and embrace all things which Christ brought us. When we have done our best toward this goal, God will empower us to withstand evil even when it is at its peak of strength. 1 Corinthians 6:7 says, *"By the word of truth, by the power of God, by the armour of righteousness on the right hand and on the left."* And if we have obtained the armour God offers, He promises that we will withstand the evil at the end of days. Ephesians 6:13 tells us, *"Wherefore take unto you the whole armour of God, that ye may be able to withstand in the evil day, and having done all, to stand."*

"Daddy", Lorraine asked, "What happens when Satan comes to us and we didn't do all these things?

"He can put fear into our hearts or cause us to stumble. And in time, he can make us lose our faith."

"Daddy", Lorraine then asked, "What happens when Satan comes to us and we did do all these things?

"Well, he cannot touch us, honey....he cannot overwhelm us because God and His angels will surround us and protect us and bring us through all things."

So when Satan struck again, Ann and Caleb were well prepared. All they had to do was trust and do their best to weather the storm. But, then again, that was easier said than done. What was to happen was indeed frightening.... for Satan struck where it really hurt......in the pocketbook!! Satan struck by feeding the fears which Ann and Caleb had just worked so hard to master. This was to be their ultimate test.

Ann and Caleb had been reading the Bible and were discussing parts of the book of Revelation. They'd asked Andrew and Lorraine if they wanted to join them and they were so excited to become a part of this ritual which their Mom and Dad performed for about a half hour each day.

Today's discussion had been about the First Resurrection and who would be taken when Christ returned.

In Revelation 7:13 they'd read, *"......What are these which are arrayed in white robes? And whence came they?"* Revelation 7:14 answered this question by saying, *"....These are they which came out of great tribulation, and have washed their robes, and made them white in the blood of the Lamb."* They spoke about how a white robe is the symbol of an unblemished soul which has had its sins forgiven and strives to do as God asks. Andrew had added that he'd been taught that the words "The blood of the Lamb" is the sacrifice which Christ made so those sins could be forgiven.

Caleb explained that the word "washing" is indicative of two processes, the first of which requires the act of acknowledging one's sins, feeling remorse for having committed them, striving to overcome the tendency to commit them again, and succeeding in much of that striving. The second part of the process is accepting and partaking of the sacrament of Holy Communion provided by the sacrifice of Christ.

Then Ann read in Revelation 3:5: *"He that overcometh.....shall be clothed in white raiment; and I will not blot out his name out of the book of life, but I will confess his name before my Father, and before his angels."* She also read from Revelation 21:7 which said: *"He that overcometh shall inherit all things; and I will be his God, and he shall be my son."*

Lorraine jumped off Ann's lap, grabbed the shawl laying across the back of the couch and paraded around the room pretending that it was her white gown. Andrew joined in the fun by placing a throw pillow across his chest saying "And I am wearing the armour of God.... no one can harm me!"

And so, their day began with a happy heart and a renewed commitment to dedicate these few minutes every day to learning about God and what He told them through scripture. They were happy again.

But, unbeknownst to Ann and Caleb, and even before Caleb had entered the hospital, the corporate headquarters of the company responsible for building the mall were having their own problems. The economy was bad and some of the investors were bailing out. Worse, there was another company setting itself up to execute a corporate buy-out of the company who employed Caleb. One option Caleb's company had to avoid this was to re-organize.... and this usually meant putting a hold on all expenditures until a new plan of action was formulated and approved.

What Caleb also didn't know was that one of the considerations on the table was to sell off the land on the far end of the mall which had been set aside to house some larger restaurants, a movie theater, and a large food market chain. Scrapping these plans would save the company millions of dollars especially if they could simply sell that land to someone else. Caleb's property, the acreage which he and Ann had purchased for an apartment complex, was on the opposite side of the land which the company now wanted to sell. A shoddy construct on that land or one which did not house potential amenities for those who might choose to live in Caleb's proposed apartment complex could seriously impact rents. Caleb wanted to build a quality complex which would mean that the apartments could demand a high rent which in turn would help Caleb to repay his loans.

Thus, when Caleb went back to work two days after their fellowship and began to hear the rumors of bankruptcy and of the company failing, his fear returned with a vengeance. His first inclination was to ask God why He was allowing this to happen. Hearing himself and attuning himself to his thoughts and how they immediately blamed God, he felt ashamed. *I've just been through this*, he thought. *Haven't I learned my lesson?* He immediately asked his Heavenly Father to forgive him and told himself over and over again that whatever was to happen, his strength and heart would be where and what God wanted, not what he wanted. *Would Ann feel the same? Would she be okay with this,* he wondered?

Despite these thoughts, Caleb's heart was beating a mile a minute and he tried to calm himself by thinking about what the words of scripture had taught him. *All men are sinners and all men are susceptible to temptation. Therefore it is important for me to fully understand that Satan and his helpers are alive and well and running rampant in their quest to bring harm to the children of God. Satan is an evil entity capable of invading man, and without God I am so weak that we I succumb to such an attack. I have to realize that while I might be battling such an entity so may someone else also be battling a satanic spirit. I might respond to what someone says and does but should do so with the understanding that I should respond instead to what these spiritual entitles may cause someone to do, or say. Misunderstanding and lack of trust in God can allow me to become the pawn or plaything of these spirits.* He remembered the words in Hosea 4:6 which warns: "*My people are destroyed for lack of knowledge....*" This verse and many others throughout scripture explain that without an understanding of what God wants to teach us, we cannot know how to battle evil. Mankind can be owned and directed by satanic influence yet once free of that influence would gladly change their lives. For this reason, we grieve God when we waste our time and energy fighting the wrong battles.

Caleb told himself that he must be on guard against the fears and lies evil tells us which distract us from the real issue we must face which is our trust in God no matter what. *Satan loves the anonymity of working in secret to keep Christians from God. He wants us to hate and judge and condemn... not Satan but God. He is so subtle that many cannot believe that he exists.* Caleb also remembered that Genesis 3:1 taught: "*..... the serpent was more subtil* *than any beast......"* That Matthew 4:1 said: *"...... to be tempted of the devil."* And in Matthew 4: 3 *"and when the tempter came to Him,....."* He also remembered that 2 Thessalonians 2:9 said: "......*Satan with all power and signs and lying wonders.*

Sure enough, later that afternoon Caleb was called to the attorney's office to meet with a number of executives from corporate headquarters. Before leaving, Caleb phoned Ann only to tell her that he had to be at a meeting and didn't know what time he'd be home but that he would phone as soon as the meeting was over. He didn't yet mention what he suspected. *Why worry her until I have all the facts. Why let her go through the anxiety I myself am feeling right now despite my determination to trust God?*

Caleb prayed. *Dear God,* he said, *here we are again and this time I can see where I have to make a decision. I have to let go in my heart of everything I once thought important to me and decide that whatever....whatever You decide for my life...and the life of my family....will be not only okay with us...but gladly accepted by us. We love you and want to decide with our heart and mind to accept Your will. Our bodies may balk, but Father don't let that stop our spiritual growth. Help me Father for I am weak. Help me Father to do the right thing to remain faithful and to be an example to my family.*

There were eight men in the attorney's conference room. Their spokesman began by talking about their main concern....the numbers.....the costs, expenses, losses, profits, etc. He went on to describe the plan which had been approved by the banks and the board of directors and by which they would all now abide. The piece of land upon which they originally hoped to build a giant food market, the movie theaters, the restaurants, and an office building, was to be sold. The remaining aspects of their current building project would remain the same. Personnel would not change, but they were moving the completion date of the mall up so they could meet the financial obligations which had been placed on them. That was it. They were dismissed.

Caleb tried to be thankful that he still had his job. In terms of his property and its future....well.... he had time to sort that out. It was a blow to learn that the property next to his would be sold and that no one could predict what would be built on that land. Caleb knew that he had to stay focused on the positive and bring that positive attitude home to Ann. He had to set the example. He didn't want to mess up this time and not give to God all that he wanted to give. He wanted to get it right this time.

Suddenly Caleb realized that perhaps fear could be a part of faith. He saw that his fear represented what he must control......and finally subdue..... in order to prove his faith.... to himself. Not to God, for God could read his heart....but to himself....and to Ann. Without the fear what else would he ever have to offer God? With the fear, he could sacrifice something. *Did that make any sense?* And as Caleb thought of this challenge he began to feel better. He wasn't fighting some intangible as he had before. He felt that perhaps he now had a better grasp about what he had to fight and what that fight was for. It made everything somehow easier to face. He could face his Goliath if he trusted God. And so with a happier, more accepting attitude, Caleb went home to tell Ann what had happened.

He decided to stop for some flowers, maybe some chocolates and maybe even a bottle of Ann's favorite wine. The children would probably be in bed, and even though he was late, Ann would have kept his dinner hot in the warming oven. If she followed their usual routine for when he was late, she'd sit at the table with him and sip a cup of tea as he ate. He thought of her loving nature and prayed that God would help her accept this latest news.

Ann was so surprised and so pleased with the flowers and chocolates, and decided to open the wine so they could share it while Caleb ate. "What's the occasion Caleb? Did you buy a new car, a new sound system, flirt with a pretty girl and feel guilty, or is it that you think it's our anniversary and you forgot it?" she teased him.

"All of the above!" he relied as he smiled at her….."But most of all, just because I love you….and even bigger than most of all…. because I have some good news for you….although…..it's disguised as bad news!"

"What? Good news disguised as bad? Now what could that mean?"

"Well, I had a sort of epiphany today Ann. It was as if the Holy Spirit was teaching me….telling me that we should welcome our tests….because we *will* pass them and *will* send Satan packing. While I already understood that our fear is induced by Satan, I suddenly understood that Satan's access to us through those fears occurs because we do not fully comprehend how much God really, really loves us. We don't fully understand that kind of love and our selfish nature causes us to be afraid that God will take something away from us despite knowing that He loves to give His children their heart's desire. We don't accept that what He *must* take *is for our own good.* But I also realized that we can use our fear as a gift to God. I mean....well.... what can we give Him? We have nothing. However, the fear we have comes from Satan, but what if we don't allow that fear to harm us and can therefore give it *purposefully and untouched...unused....* to God. Wouldn't that prove our determination to overcome? I'm probably not making myself clear here.......what I'm trying to say is that if we accept our fear as a fact *but...*we don't allow it to influence our actions, we win, Satan loses, and God smiles!"

"You mean not fear our fear?"

"Yes Ann...that's it....well said....that's it exactly. If we don't fear our fear, but let it flow over us, and not enter us, it can't hurt us, and we can place our focus on trusting God entirely with our life."

"Caleb, what is it that you are not telling me? There *is* something that you haven't told me isn't there?"

"Yes…but I know in my heart that the final outcome will be what's right for us….can you believe that too?"

"You lost your job."

"No. I still have and will have my job. But, the company is having some financial problems because of the downturn in the economy and is therefore re-organizing. They are going to sell the piece of property next to the mall where they originally planned to build the giant supermarket, the movie theaters, the office suites, and the larger restaurants. That property, as you know, is next to the one we recently purchased. Our only fear is…with this bad economy…if they let it go cheap and someone builds something on that land which is less than top rate or…….worse yet, builds an apartment complex which could compete with the apartments we'd like to build on the adjacent lot…then our property and our plans may not be the benefit we'd hoped."

"Oh Caleb, we've sunk every penny into that property and now have no idea whether or not we will even get our money back."

"Ann, like I said, let's use our fears…let's look at our fear, acknowledge it….and give it to God.   We have to Ann….we have to….we want to pass this test of faith…right?"

"Oh Caleb, of course we do….but this is so hard, this is so frightening…..we have children…. we have this house and all its expenses…we have the mortgage on the new property. Oh Caleb, what will we do?"

"Ann that's just it……we do nothing…we sit….we pray….we trust God….we turn our fears over to Him….and we do *not* let Satan   turn our fear into something he can use against us….in other words….*we win this battle by trusting that what happens will be for our good.*"

"Can we do this Caleb? Can I? I want to…..ohh, how I want to…..but I think about the children and I….."

"Ann, turn even the children over to God and let Him decide what path our lives will take. I'm scared too, but if we *both* decide to do this…together….we can….we will….and we will be better for it. Deal?"

"Deal, if you are okay with this, then I am too," Ann replied and moved into Caleb's lap for comfort.

"Whenever we feel the fear, we'll pray together and we will support one another through any news…good or bad….and give God time to take this where He wants it."

"Okay Caleb, I know that you are right and that God will help us….and to tell you the truth it's almost a relief not to have to worry…to let go and to let God."

"I'll bet Ann that in six months time we will be smiling again!"

Chapter Twelve

GOD'S PLAN FOR ALL MEN

One day, a few weeks later Ann arrived home from shopping to find ten men in the family room. She'd been out looking for a pair of shoes to match a new dress Lorraine had received as a gift. The men had all come to the house to help remove the fallen branch and prune the tree in the back yard which had been struck by lightning that day of Caleb's accident. They also meticulously cut and stacked the wood for Caleb's fireplace. As Ann walked into the family room she saw ten happy men sprawled all over the floor, careful not to dirty the upholstery with their sweaty clothing. Matt was talking, evidently answering a question which one of the men had raised. Ann leaned against the doorway and happily listened. She hoped that they would not even notice her and would go on with their conversation.

"It is almost impossible to know what God asks of us, or develop the kind of heart God loves if we do not know the word of God and thus understand what we must be aware of, and how we can fight the forces which work to keep us from becoming all that God hopes. And if we do have an enemy who has the power to keep us from God and the power to cause us to behave in an ungodly manner, why would we *not* want to learn how to do battle with this enemy? Can we fight an enemy we don't know exists? After all, he's a strong, powerful, supernatural entity who was once sitting next to God. He must destroy us to stay free and he has minions of helpers to do so. He knows scripture and God's plan of salvation, and therefore fully understands that when God finds the number of souls He longs for, he will no longer have a reason to tempt mankind, and will soon be bound for one thousand years."

Josh jumped in to the conversation adding: "Yeah, what Matt says is right and when Satan left heaven, he took one third of all the angels God originally created with him to work against us. They have the power to enter and dwell in us and prevent us from seeking God. We must realize that this is something to be feared, and in that fear we must learn of this enemy and how to protect ourselves and our loved ones. Satan and his helpers want to destroy the faith of the children of God, thus God warns us in Luke 11:26, *"Then goeth he, and taketh to him seven other spirits more wicked than himself; and they enter in, and dwell there: and the last state of that man is worse than the first."*

Caleb then added, "This is a clear warning that the spirits of evil can enter our hearts and dwell there causing incredible havoc in our lives and separation from God. But if we are faithful, if we learn God's words and direction, we find that no matter what we face, God provides for us. God comforts us with the words from Luke 11:11-13 which tell us, *"If a son shall ask bread of any of you that is a father, will he give a stone.......how much more shall your Heavenly Father give the Holy Spirit to them that ask him?* You know Guys, Ann and I almost succumbed to the fear and anger Satan instilled in us just from the *potential* of losing our health, thus our job, our home, everything material. We had to struggle to get back on track! We needed to re-visit God's words to know God, know what He tells us, what evil we face, and what God offers us.....and ask Him to help us. If ignorance of the law is not reason enough to be excused from error in our courts and judicial system, why would it be a reason to be excused for our sins and excused for our refusal to learn God's words and strive to please Him in the spiritual system?"

Wade, not to be outdone explained, "Right...there *is* no excuse. When Adam and Eve sinned by disobeying God, they opened the door to the curse which required mankind to learn about evil. But God arranged that by learning of evil, mankind could also learn to appreciate what is good, and from that experience, have the opportunity to choose God and His ways... and spurn all evil. The curse which resulted from the disobedience of Adam and Eve separated man from God. Called *inherited sin*, it is why God provided the sacrament of Baptism. God also provided the forgiveness of sin and the Holy Spirit to help mankind overcome the influence of Satan. Thus all men are sinners and only through the sacrifice of Christ can those sins be forgiven and thus again allow man fellowship with God.

Scripture also addresses the sins of our forefathers which is similar to inherited sin because it too is passed from generation to generation. This may be why some families never escape certain family patterns such as the alcoholism which may occur in a grandfather, a father and a son. Only when we ask and then allow God to cleanse us and we take on the fight to overcome those patterns or tendencies can we break free. This is why God speaks over and over again in scripture about being an overcomer, fighting the good fight, watching for our enemy, and praying for and loving one another."

All eyes then turned to Jim who'd not too many years ago struggled to become a believer. Jim was saying: "Keeping God first and foremost in our lives is paramount to freeing ourselves from satanic ownership and passing that ownership to our children through our sins. A great example of this is how we have always been blessed as a country because we've kept God in everything, from school prayer, to the décor of our government buildings, even to our currency. Now, we are losing that blessing because a few are banning all acknowledgement and worship of God in public buildings. Therefore, what had been passed down as a *blessing* from our ancestors is turning into a *curse* for future generations because we are taking God out of the equation. We are witnessing the *generational sins of the forefathers* quite clearly as we witness the loss of faith, the loss of family values, the drug abuse, alcoholism, a corrupt government and a myriad of other problems going from grandfather to father to child. Even many ungodly activities are now being accepted as a "disease" or a part of one's DNA which cannot nor should not be overcome, instead of the sin that it is But the truth is that Satan is the father of a host of actions and attitudes which rob us of our blessings, our faith, our peace and our relationship with God. Without God's protection and what we must learn which will help us fight evil, we could lose not only our blessings, but our entire future with God. It's mind boggling what the unbelievers of this generation are throwing away. Matthew 23:33 warns, *"Ye serpents, ye generation of vipers, how can ye escape the damnation of hell?"* Ezekiel 31:16 warns, *"I made the nations to shake at the sound of his fall, when I cast him down to hell with them that descend into the pit . . ."* This verse tells us that not only will Satan be cast into hell but others with him as well. These include the evil spirits who were thrown from heaven with Satan because they too rebelled against God. But also included will be the "goats" who scripture describes as those who would not accept what God both offered and required. Therefore, it could be us unless we put God first in our lives."

Joe then asked, "But what is all this struggle for...I mean what is the outcome...why do we have to go through all this?"

John, the eldest of the men, tried to explain. "Well Joe, as we read scripture, the beautiful plan which begins and ends with God's desire for the future of mankind is unveiled for us. God, knowing that man would sin, arranged for him to learn of good and evil so he would have the opportunity to freely choose good, to repent of all evil, and to seek the forgiveness of his sin and a life with God. Scripture teaches us that God longs to fill His new kingdom with souls who will truly love one another, and love His Son and Him above all things. Matthew 22:37-39 says, *"Jesus said unto him, Thou shalt love the Lord thy God with all thy heart, and with all thy soul, and with all thy mind. This is the first and great commandment. And the second is like unto it, Thou shalt love thy neighbor as thyself."* God wants these souls to understand the value of love, trust, and loyalty, and to practice these attributes voluntarily. (John

14:23) God began His plan by creating the earth in its limited universe. Then He created Adam and Eve to live happily in the Garden of Eden, walking and talking with Him. But the angel Lucifer, later known as Satan, rebelled against God because he was jealous of Christ, and of the new being, man, who God planned to elevate above the angels. (Isaiah 14:12-15) As a result of his rebellion, Satan was thrown to earth with the angels (Revelation 12:9) who followed Satan and thereby also disobeyed God. These numbered one-third of all the angels. Satan knew God's plan and understood that when the plan was completed, and God had obtained the number of faithful loving souls He longed for, Satan would be thrown into Hell for what he had done and with him *all* evil would be forever bound. To prevent God's plan from moving forward and thus forestall his own destruction, Satan destroyed God's relationship of trust and loyalty with Adam and Eve by enticing them to sin through disobedience. Satan knew that sin would automatically separate man from God because of God's perfect righteousness. Thus, God then had to banish Adam and Eve as he had banished Satan. (Genesis 3:1 and Genesis 3:23) But God, knowing what Satan would do, provided a way for Adam and Eve, and the generations to follow, to escape the captivity of Satan through the forgiveness of sin and return to God. In fact, this is why Christ offered Himself as the perfect sacrifice by which the sins of man could be forgiven. (John 1:29) At every turn, Satan interfered with God's plan, trying to destroy those who tried to follow God. He knew that when God collected the number of souls He desired for His new creation, Satan would be bound forever. Thus Satan is fighting for his life when trying to draw us into sin. However, because of God's love, many of those tested by Satan are strengthened through his attacks, becoming like gold refined in the fires of tribulation. From these faithful, God is building what the Bible calls The Bride of Christ. God also provided for those who died in sin both before and after Christ provided His sacrifice by creating a means of testimony in eternity. Thus while grace is still available on earth, it is also available in eternity. Christ entered hell after His death to give testimony of His triumph to those who had died in their sins before He could bring His perfect sacrifice. (Luke 24:46) He told them that now they too could find forgiveness. (1Timothy 2:4) A specific amount of time has been allotted in God's Plan of Salvation for His chosen ones to be made ready. (Acts 1:6-7) When that time is up, God will send His Son back to earth for the First

Resurrection (Revelation 20:5) when He will take to heaven both those from eternity who have obtained forgiveness and those alive who have remained faithful. (2Peter 3:10) When they are gone, grace will also be gone, and the final destruction of the end times will begin on the earth where, among other things, one-third of all the people on earth will die. When the destruction ends, God will send His Son back to earth with those He had taken at the First Resurrection. They will have celestial (perfect) bodies, and will reign as kings and priests for one thousand years of peace to bring testimony to everyone living or dead who was not taken in the First Resurrection.

Satan will be bound during this time, unable to influence mankind, so all of mankind will learn about and accept God. But, after the one thousand years of peace, Satan will be loosed again for a little while so those who have now accepted God can be tested. (Revelation 20:7) Satan will wreak havoc on those not firm in their faith and many will leave God and follow him. (Revelation 20:2) Then the Day of Judgment will arrive when *everyone* who was ever born, or conceived, except those taken by Christ for the First Resurrection, *will be judged.* Some of these people, which the Bible calls the "goats", will be cast into hell with Satan forever, while others, called the "lambs", will inhabit God's new kingdom where there will be no sorrow and no tears. The goats, and Satan and his angels, will be cast into the lake of fire and brimstone and tormented day and night forever. (Revelation 20:10 and 15) Those who are taken for the First Resurrection will continue to reign as kings and priests in the new kingdom to live in the City of God. They will never have to be judged because their sins were forgiven, and entirely wiped away by God. Also important for us to know is that God wants a specific number of souls to be a part of the Bride of Christ. This is mentioned in scripture and also mentioned in the Apocrypha. 11 Esdras 2:40-41 says, *"Receive they number O Sion, and embrace those of thine that are clothed in white which have fulfilled the law of the Lord. The number of thy children whom thou longest for, is fulfilled: beseech the Lord that thy people, which have been called from the beginning, may be hallowed."* Our desire as Christians is to work toward the completion of God's work here on earth, labor in faith, love, and charity to make ourselves worthy to be a child of God. We learn God's words, put on the armor of God, seek forgiveness, strive to be an overcomer, and wait patiently for the completion of God's Plan of Salvation and the return of His Son. We carry the hope in our hearts that soon God will find the last soul. Romans 8:25 tells us, "*But if we hope for that we see not, then do we with patience wait for it.*"

"Gee whiz, I never heard all that before" Joe replied. "So there *is* a plan and if I want in, I'd better get on board."

"You're almost on board already Joe, you just don't realize it....I mean...coming to church with us, listening to us talk.....believing what we say....you are almost there.....you just have to actually give your "yes word" to God!" Wade laughed...."Ya know, like gettin' married!"

The men all laughed again and, suddenly noticing Ann standing at the entry listening to them, they all said hello. Ann moved from the doorway to sit on the hearth and when she had a cup of tea in her hand, she turned to Caleb and asked him if he'd told the others about the availability of the property adjacent to the mall. Ann suggested that he tell them now because she had an idea which might be of interest to all of them.

So, Caleb began to tell the men what he'd recently learned about the future plans which the company who was currently building the mall had just announced. When he was finished, Ann began to speak: "Jim and Wade you are large scale commercial contractors and architects, Joe and Preacher you both work for contractors. Josh has also done lots of construction work. Kevin, Richard, and Matt, you all know quite a bit about banking and investments, and John.... you had an accounting firm for years......so why not pool your resources and buy that property? Especially knowing that it's a sale which *needs* to be made...therefore which might be a *bargain*!"

"Ann, what a great idea!" Caleb exclaimed.

The men were immediately engaged and excited. What a great project that would be, even if they only bought the property and later re-sold it after the mall was completed or even after Caleb's apartments had been built. The property would surely show well then!

An hour later the men were still talking about the potential of such a venture and how many others they could get to form the company which would purchase this land. Ann had to shoo them home so their wives wouldn't come looking for them!

As this idea began to formulate, Richard brought in another physician investor and his brother-in-law who was a commercial realtor who was best known for his negotiating skills. Richard's brother-in-law did his homework and learned what the bottom line was for the banks to re-coup their investment and for the company to be off the hook for future payments. The property was now going to be offered as a short sale and the bank hoped for a bidding war. However, having prior knowledge about what permits would be allowed and what would not, their offer contained the least restrictions and offered the fastest closing date and therefore the bank took notice of their offer. In the end, the negotiated price was nothing short of miraculous.

The men were overjoyed and looked forward to what the future would bring in regard to this new investment. They had many options in front of them: They could re-sell the property; they could build on it and then sell it; they could build to rent; they could expand on Caleb's plans for his own property. They could enjoy the camaraderie of coming up with many different ideas for the project. It seemed that another fellowship was in order and the group rejoiced and thanked God for what God had brought them and the miracle of a problem becoming a great blessing!

Later, when Ann and Caleb sat together in the family room they began to talk about the events of the past few days and how they would never have guessed how God would answer their prayers! Ann said: "You were right Caleb....even fear can become a blessing if we give it to God and don't allow it to touch our faith."

Caleb replied saying, "Ann, we have been so blessed because we have seen firsthand how God *always* brings us through *everything*! How exciting that soon, our entire group of family and friends will be embarking on yet another venture which might also test our faith, but can build our future, and strengthen our relationships. And all we have to do is try our best to live according to God's will and trust Him!"

"Yes Caleb, but this time, we will have a better understanding of the need to avoid thinking that we are already "okay" spiritually and that we must acknowledge the absolute need to ask God to help us see our shortcomings and not let us fall into complacency about where we might be on our spiritual growth ladder!"

"Yup…true, and we'd better be sure to watch for Satan and how subtly he works in our natural lives…*through fear of loss especially*…..and we'd better try harder to trust God when things appear to go wrong!"

"Oh Caleb, can we? Will we?"

"Yes Ann, because we will pray, we will try harder to look for the blessing in *everything*, even the bad stuff, and we will all support one another in this quest. And now we have learned to look more deeply into our hearts so we can learn what *really* lives there. We will ask ourselves: Are we selfish, are we too attached to our material possessions, are we getting complacent, do we really put God above everything we have and love and know?"

So, Ann and Caleb prayed, thanked God and asked Him to help them see His hand of grace in everything and always be thankful for His blessings and to always want to look inside themselves to learn where they still needed correction.

And God smiled!

Scriptural Index

1 John 2:16 *"….. the lust of the eyes… pride of life, is not of the Father, but of the world.."* 113

1 Timothy 3:6 *"….lest being lifted up with pride he fall into the condemnation of the devil."* 113

11 Cor. 12:7-11 *"….there was given to me a thorn in the flesh….lest I should be exalted."* 114

Matthew 7:3-5 *"…why beholdest …the mote in thy brothers eye, but….not the beam in thine own…."* 114

Romans 8:28 *"All things work together for the good of those that love the Lord."* 126

Philippians 4:19 *""And the peace of God…. shall keep your hearts and minds through Christ."* 127

John 14:27 *"Peace I leave with you, my peace I give unto you; Let not your heart be troubled…"* 127

Philippians 4:13 *"I can do all things through Christ which strengtheneth me"* 127

Mark 14:34 *"My soul is exceedingly sorrowful unto death."* 130, 131

Mark 14:36 *"Father,….. Take this cup from me, nevertheless not what I will but what thou will."* 131

Mark 14:39 *"..and again He went away and prayed, and spoke the same words."* 131

Matthew 11:28 *"Come unto me, all ye that labour and are heavy laden, and I will give you rest."* 138

Philippians 4:13 *"I can do all things through Christ which strengtheneth me."* 139

Philippians 4:19 *"But my God shall supply all your need….."* 139

11 Timothy 1:7 *"For God hath not given us the spirit of fear; but of power, and of love…."* 139

Hebrews 13:5   *".... be without covetousness; and be content....I will never leave thee, nor forsake thee." 139*

Matthew 25:21   *".... thou hast been faithful over a few things. I will make thee ruler over many things..." 140*

Matthew 25:10-12 *".... they that were ready went; and the door was shut. ... the other.... I know you not." 140*

1 Cor 15:58   *"Therefore, be ye abounding in the work of the Lord...... your labour in not in vain." 141*

John 17:24, 25   *"Father, I will that they be with me, behold my glory, known that thou hast sent me." 160*

Matthew 6:7   *"... when ye pray, use not repetitions as the heathen: for they think they shall be heard ...." 161. 162*

Matthew 7:7   *"Ask and it shall be given; seek, and ye shall find; knock, and it shall be opened unto you." 162, 163*

Matthew 6:26   *"....the birds... neither sow nor reap nor gather; yet your heavenly Father feedeth them." 163, 164*

Matthew 10:29, 31 *"...two sparrows... shall not fall without your Father....Fear ye not therefore..." 164*

Matthew 6:5   *"... when thou prayest, be not as the hypocrites: they love to pray...that they may be seen..." 164*

James 1:5   *"If any of you lack wisdom, let him ask of God, that giveth liberally, and it shall be given." 165*

Deut. 11:13-14:   *".... love the Lord... serve Him... that I will give you the ..... rain, corn, wine, and oil." 165*

Psalm 133:1   *"Behold, how good and how pleasant it is for brethren to dwell together in unity!" 181*

Colossians 3:21 *"Fathers, provoke not your children to anger, lest they be discouraged." 182*

Hebrews 13:6   ... *we may boldly say, The Lord is my helper, and I will not fear what man shall do unto me". 182*

Hebrews 13:16   *"But do good and to communicate forget not; for with such sacrifices God is well pleased." 182*

Matthew 7:12   *"Therefore all things whatsoever ye would that men do to you, do ye even so to them...." 182*

Proverbs 16:24   *"Pleasant words are as a honeycomb; sweet to the soul, and health to the bones." 182*

Proverbs 8:32   *"....for blessed are they that keep my ways." 182*

Eccles 12:14   *"For God shall bring every work into judgment, with every secret .... good, or...evil" 183*

Proverbs 29:23   *"A man's pride shall bring him low...." 186*

1 John 2:16   *".... the lust of flesh and eyes, and pride of life, is not of the Father, but is of the world." 186*

Mark 13:20   *"And except that the Lord hath shortened, those days, no flesh should be saved..." 192*

1 Peter 4:7   *"But the end of all things is at hand; be ye therefore sober, and watch unto prayer." 193*

1 Peter 5:8   *"Be sober, vigilant,....the devil... walketh about, seeking who he may devour." 193*

John 14:27   *"Peace I give you: not as the world giveth.. Let not your heart be troubled, afraid." 195*

2 Cor. 2:11   *"Lest Satan get an advantage." 196.*

Proverbs 3:34   *"He scorneth the scorners: but he giveth grace unto the lowly." 200*

Matthew 25:21   *".....thou hast been faithful over a few things, I will make thee ruler over many..." 205*

1 Cor. 13:11   *"When I was a child, I understood as a child.... but when a man, put away childish things."* 205

Revelation 2:11   *"....He that overcometh shall not be hurt in the second death."*   205

Revelation 2:26   *"And he that overcometh and keepeth my works will I give power over the nations."* 205

Revelation 3:5   *"He that overcometh,shall be clothed in white...I will .. confess his name before my Father,"*   205. 206

Revelation 21:7   *"He that overcometh shall inherit all things; and I will be his God, and he shall be my son."* 206

Revelation 7:13   *"...... What are these which are arrayed in white robes? And whence came they?"* 206

Revelation 7:14   *"....they which came out of great tribulation, washed their robes, in the blood of the Lamb."* 206

Romans 12:2,   *"Be ye transformed that ye may prove what is that good and perfect will of God."* 207

Galatians 5:1   *"Be ye not entangled again with the yoke of bondage."* 207

Ephesians 6:11   *"Put on the armour of God, that ye may be able to stand against the wiles of the devil."* 207, 208

Romans 13:12   *"The day is at hand; cast off the works of darkness and let us put on the armour of light."* 208

1 Cor. 6:7   *"By the word of truth, the power of God, the armour of righteousness......"* 209

Ephesians 6:13   *"....take unto you the armour of God, that ye may be able to withstand the evil....."* 209

Hosea 4:6:   *"My people are destroyed for lack of knowledge; rejected knowledge, I will reject thee ..."* 212

Genesis 3:1   " the serpent was more subtil than any beast..." 212, 213

Matthew 4:1   "Then was Jesus led. be tempted of the devil." 213

Matthew 4: 3   "and when the tempter came to Him, he said.." 213

2 Thess 2:9   "......the working of Satan with all power and signs and lying wonders." 213

Luke 11:26   "Then goeth he, and taketh seven other spirits more wicked than himself; and they enter... " 223

Luke 11:11-13   "If a son ask bread of a father, will he give a stone..... more your Heavenly Father gives" 223

Matthew 23:33   "Ye serpents, ye generation of vipers, how can ye escape the damnation of hell?" 226

Ezekiel 31:16   "...the nations shake at the sound of his fall, when I cast him down to hell ..." 226

Matt. 22:37-39   "....love the Lord...with all thy heart, and soul, and mind... love thy neighbor as thyself." 227

John 14:23   "If a man love me and keep my words, my Father will love him...make our abode with him." 227

Isaiah 14:12-15   "..Lucifer. Thou hast said, I will exalt my throne....yet thou shalt be brought down to hell...." 227

Revelations 12:9   "..that old drgon called the Devil, and Satan...was cast out into the earth and his angels.." 227

Genesis 3:1   "Now the serpent was more subtil than any beast which the Lord had made...."   228

Genesis 3:23   "Therefore the Lord God sent him forth from the garden of Eden to till the ground...." 228

John 1:29   "Behold the lamb of God which taketh away the sin of the world." 228

Luke 24:46   *"...It is written...thus it behooved Christ to suffer and to rise from the dead the third day." 229*

1 Timothy 2:4   *"Who will have all men to be saved, and to come unto the knowledge of the truth." 229*

Acts 1:6-7   *"Lord wilt thou at this time restore the kingdom to Israel....It is not for you to know the time" 229*

Revelation 20:5 *"..the rest of the dead lived not again until the thousand years were finished...." 229*

11 Peter 3:10   *"The day of the Lord will come as a thief in the night.... the heavens will pass away..." 229*

Revelation 20:7 *"And when the thousand years ar expired, Satan shall be loosed out of his prison." 230*

Revelation 20:2 *"...he laid hold on the Devil...Satan...and bound him a thousand years." 230*

Rev. 20:10, 15   *"...the devil...into the lake of fire, tormented and those not in the book of life." 230*

11 Esdras 2:40-41 *"Receive thy number... The number thou longest for, is fulfilled....." 230, 231*

Romans 8:25   *"But if we hope for that we see not, then do we with patience wait for it." 231*

Luke 11:11-13,   *"If a son ask bread of a father,will he give a stone... more shall your Heavenly Father give." 252*

Bibliography

The Holy Bible, King James Version, published by The New Apostolic Church, Canada, Thomas Nelson, Inc., Camden, NJ, 1972

James Strong, LLD, STD, *Strong's Exhaustive Concordance of the Bible*, Abington, Nashville, thirty fourth printing 1996, copyright 1890

Henry H. Halley, *Halley's Bible Handbook,* Zondervan Publishing House, Grand Rapids, Michigan, 24th edition, Copyright 1965

Henry M. Morris, *Many Infallible Proofs*, Moody Press, Chicago, 3rd printing 1977

Henry M. Morris, *The Bible and Modern Science*, Moody Press, Chicago, 1951, 1968

Donald Grey Barnhouse, *The Invisible War,* Zondervan Publishing House, Grand Rapids, Michigan, 12th printing 1976 copyright 1965

Robert Boyd, *Boyd's Bible Handbook*, Eugene, Oregon: Harvest House, 1983

Websters New Ninth Collegiate Dictionary, Mirriam-Webster, 1986

Roget's II The New Thesaurus, Houghton Mifflin Company, Boston, 1980, by the editors of *The American Heritage Dictionary.*

About The Author

Helen Glowacki is an interior designer, writer, teacher, and motivational speaker. She was the host, writer, and producer of the television series "The Contemporary Woman", broadcast by UA Columbia Cablevision. Her writing credentials include an extensive background as a freelance feature and staff writer for four newspapers and for various newsletters and magazines.

A graduate of William Paterson University, Helen received a Bachelor of Arts degree, magna cum laude, in Communications. She also received an Associate of Science degree with honors and is a registered nurse.

Helen donates her books to cancer centers, drug rehabilitation centers, and prisons. She also donates them to the mission schools of *The Henwood Foundation* to use her gift for writing to help others find the love and comforting presence of God. Helen gladly emails one of her mini-books to those who wish help her bring testimony to others. Helen has written a number of well received Christian articles which are filed with insight about scripture and how God wants us to conduct our lives. She posts many of these on Face Book and on her website

Those who have provided reviews of Helen's books tout the beautiful stories in her novels and her non-fiction books as spiritually uplifting and biblically correct. Her greatest joys are her husband, two children, four grandchildren, and time spent in her New Apostolic faith and in fellowship.

For more information:

Visit the author's website at: www.helenglowacki.com or visit Amazon.com. You can also email the author at: helen@helenglowacki.com

Excerpt from the book "Do Our Little Sins Really Count?"

Most of us believe that it's the large sins which God will count and that it's simply human nature to commit the smaller sins. Yet scripture tells us that God seeks those who will be a perfect bride for His Son. But the reality is that just as our spouse, children, and friends may be well aware of our faults, and want us to overcome them. so too would the bridegroom with whom we hope to share our future.

Thus perhaps our little sins *are* important and that whatever we do, say and think should be examined in the light of how the Lord Jesus would look upon them. While we are assured that we will be forgiven our sins when the Lord returns for His Bride, we may not be forgiven for the sins for which we have no remorse.

Scripture describes those who Christ will take at the First Resurrection as "overcomers". This word infers that we have done the work to uncover our sins and strive to "go and sin no more". Therefore it is our *striving* and our hearts attitude toward sin which matters most. Matthew 25:21 promises: *".....thou hast been faithful over a few things, I will make thee ruler over many..."*

Do Our Little Sins Really Count is the sixth book in the "Why God Why" mini-series by Helen Glowacki. These non-fiction series of books are written in an easy to understand manner and consist of only 126 pages each, yet are packed full of information for those who seek to learn more about God's plan for them.

It is another must read for those who may not have the time to read scripture yet desire to understand what God tells us and how His words of instruction relates to their future.

List and Description of Novels
by Helen Glowacki
(Book Size 6 x 9)

When God Broke Grandma's Heart: (208 pages) Rising from sorrow to become a beacon of faith Grandma struggles in an abusive marriage until God moves her from unequally yoked and broken to the healing of His love and forgiveness. Her granddaughter Sarah learns where to find answers to her problems and carries that legacy to those she loves. **Paperback: ISBN 978-0-9847-2110-8**

When God Took Grandma Home: (260 pages) About the heartache of drug addiction, of the enemy who destroys children through drugs, why God allows righteous anger, why we should pray for those in eternity and a description an incredible experience of faith for Matt and Sarah about why God allowed such heartache to occur. **Paperback: ISBN 978-0-49847-2111-5**

When Grandma Chased the Spirits: (208 Pages) The magnetism of idolatry, it's invisible power, and the heartache of bearing a child out of wedlock brings debilitating panic attacks to Mary and affects her husband Kevin. When Matt and Sarah tell them about their faith, God engineers a miracle to solve what that they thought impossible to resolve. **Paperback: ISBN 978-0-9847-2112-2**

The Granddaughter and the Monkey Swing: (284 pages) A wedding, a broken engagement, renovating and decorating a home through Divine Proportion, the truth about Halloween, and the gift of role models create a tender story of friendship. Helping through the planning and problems of a wedding culminates in the unveiling of a secret. **Paperback: ISBN 978-0- 9847-2113-9**

Grandma's Little Book of Poetry: The Story of God's Plan of Salvation: (277 pages) This beautiful whimsical story for all ages, begins when Sarah finds a manuscript in Grandma's desk and recognizes the story Grandma read to her and Josh and Caleb when they were children. Angels watch the inhabitants below them struggle to find God. **Paperback: ISBN 978-0-9847-2114-6**

Abiding Faith, Hidden Treasure: (262 pages) Serving in Iraq, Jim loses his faith to see a loving God allow so much heartache. Barbara invites him to dinner where Grandma shows him why creation and evolution co-exist and God's enemy creates the injustices Jim blames on God. Letters from the grave bring an incredible experience of faith. **Paperback: ISBN 978-0-9847-2115-3**

And Then They Asked God: (295 Pages) When Rebecca and Jayden arrive at their college campus they are overwhelmed by betrayal. Losing the values Rebecca once cherished fills her with guilt so monumental that she cannot forgive herself. Chaldeth the evil angel is defeated when God's grace frees Jayden and brings Rebecca's recovery. **Paperback: ISBN 978-0-9847-2116-7**

Caleb's Testimony: (262 pages) Caleb would have taken bets on his ability to trust God explicitly....until his accident.. Now, he and Ann must face the wrath of Satan aimed at causing them to blame God for their misfortune. **Paperback: ISBN 978-0-9847-2119-1.**

List of the "Why God Why" mini-series by Helen Glowacki

(Book Size 5 ½ x 8)

To What Purpose?: (126 pages) This first book in the *Why God Why* series answers questions about why we are here, what we need to learn, and what God plans for us. It is an excellent book for testimony and one you will share with others.

Paperback: ISBN 978-1-4507-7580-9

Why God, Why?: (126 pages) This second book in the *Why God Why* Series describes why we experience heartache, its purpose, and how to face it. It answers questions about God's plan for us and what we need to do to be found worthy.

Paperback: ISBN 978-1-4507-7581-6

Why Trust Scripture?: (126 pages) This third book in the *Why God, Why* Series addresses the challenges against scripture, who wrote the Bible, the importance of the sacraments, what role Satan plays, and how health and the Bible are related.

Paperback: ISBN 978-1-4507-7582-3

What Should I Know about Life after Death and the Coming Tribulation?: (126 pages) What occurs following death, what will happen during the tribulation, and what the seven seals could mean to us are explained in this fourth book of the series.

Paperback: ISBN 978-1-4507-7583-0

**What Does God Want Me to do Right Now**?: (126 pages) A concise explanation of what God asks of us, how we can live up to His expectations what is required to become a part of the Bride of Christ, and what God plans for the future with or without us.

Paperback: ISBN 978-1 4507-9076-5

Coming Soon

**Do The Little Sins Really Count**? (126 pages) Most of us believe that the little sins don't really matter but scripture explains why they do.

Paperback: ISBN: 978-0-9847-2117-7

List of Non-Fiction Books
By Helen Glowacki
(Book Size 5 ½ x 8 ½)

Politically Incorrect: The Get Some Gumption Handbook For When Enough is Enough: (406 pages) Fifty timely and controversial issues are examined under the politically correct approach and compared to what scripture tells us is the approach that God wants His children to take.
Paperback: ISBN 978-1-4507-9074-1

Overcoming Depression: How To Be Happy: (258 pages) We all face heartache, and all feel sad from time to time. But depression lingers and can result from many different causes. It can rob us of hope and destroy our relationship with God. Thus our Heavenly Father tells us through scripture how we can tap into His blessing and His direction and brings joy out of tribulation.
Paperback: ISBN 978-1-4507-9077-2

What No One Tells You About Addictions: (216 pages) Discussing the merits of tough love, the selfish co-dependency of the enabler, what scripture tells us about spiritual warfare and invasion, and generational sin, make this book a must read.
Paperback: ISBN 978-1- 4507--9075-8

"If a son shall ask bread

of any of you that is a father,

will he give a stone.…...

how much more shall your

Heavenly Father

give the Holy Spirit

to them that ask him?"

Luke 11:11-13

Book Reviews

Reverend (District Apostle Ret.) Richard C. Freund, President of The New Apostolic Church, USA, Sea Cliff, New York: Magnificent writer, a story which makes the reader become emotionally involved, a joy to read, strong Christian values. *"When God Broke Grandma's Heart",* best seller quality.

Reverend (District Apostle Ret.) Richard C. Freund, President of The New Apostolic Church, USA. Helen's new novel, *"When God Took Grandma Home"* "Delights, brings comfort to those who grieve. Inspires, gives insight into the after-life, masterful portrayal.

Reverend Andrew Muliokela: New Apostolic Church in Alexandria, Virginia, formerly from Zambia Africa: *The Granddaughter and the Monkey Swing* and this series of books are awesome! A journey unlike another, I was reading a great novel, learning about confidence, love and support but also learning Bible verses at the same time! Helen Glowacki teaches through her books and I recommend them 100%. You'll enjoy the journey!

Reverend Frederick Rothe, (Ret. New Apostolic Church, New York) Palm Beach Gardens Congregation, Florida: Spent 48 years serving God and another 30 in the congregation. These books contain an accurate account of what God wants of us and why we suffer. The application of scripture and the people in the stories stand for the principles God wants in all of us.

Reverend Kevin Speranza, New Apostolic Church, Palm Beach Gardens, Florida: *And Then They Asked God* so happy I read this, weaves, documents biblical precepts, addresses political correctness, moral & political corruption, biased teaching, insidious growth of socialism renamed progressivism, self-importance, guilt and its debilitating power. WELL DONE! Identifies danger, artfully and Biblically addresses them.

Reverend Luke Jansen, Sr. V. P., Medical Connections, Boca Raton, Florida: "To Ms. Glowacki, author of **The Grandma Series**: grateful for your books, refreshing to find a Christian author who sees the *difference* between religion and spirituality AND that the two can and should be used in the same sentence.

Reverend Derryck Beukes, Montana-De Aar Congregation, Northern Cape, South Africa: Dear Helen, I personally often use your articles in my soul care visits, especially where youth are involved. I can assure you that your articles made a difference to my way of thinking, and I am busy encouraging fellow priests to read your works, as they are so factual and insightful! Thank you for your hard work. I thank God for you, and the wisdom He gave you! Please continue with the excellent work.

Deacon Shadreck Wilima, Overspill Congregation, Ndola, Zambia: Your articles prompt realistic examples which New Apostolic Christians need for their everyday living.

Youth Chairperson, Sunday School Teacher, Mulenga Ernest, Lusaka Central Congregation, Lusaka, Zambia: Through your writing I am constantly reminded of what to be aware of. I pray that God keeps you in the hollow of His hand, guards you and guides you to reach your brethren as you do me. Thanks for caring for the souls of many.

Reverend Aurelio Cerullo, Atripalda Congregation in Campania, Southern Italy: Dear Helen, your books and articles, and social networking bring brothers and sisters the words of our faith and touch the hearts of those who do not know our faith. Our goal isfound through the grace of the apostolate and in this sense, the word's from 1 Corinthians 15:58 assumes an important meaning: *"Therefore, my beloved brethren, be steadfast, immovable, always abounding in the work of the Lord, Knowing That your labor is not in vain in the Lord"*. Now that I am a minister of God for about a year I too am grateful to our beloved Father in Heaven for having opened the eyes of my soul, for having removed the plugs from my ears of my heart to hear and listen to His will in connection and communion with those who precede us, guided by the light of the Holy Spirit. God's work always evolves and adapts to the times and even via computers, cell phones and smart phones. I Thank God for having been able to know you, you're a very valuable pearl. God bless you richly.

Rev. Fred Krueger, (Ret.) Lutheran Minister 12 yrs and Clinical Social Worker 26 years, Dallas, Texas: "Inspiring, grabs the heart, author headed to the bestseller list, a pleasure to read, masterful. *"When God Took Grandma Home"* filled with insight into God's plan!

NOTE: The articles which are referred to in these reviews are excerpts from Helen Glowacki's non-fiction books. Not shown are reviews by the ministers who oversee *The Henwood Foundation*'s New Apostolic Mission Schools in Zambia and review all reading materials prior to distribution.

Edith Stier, wife of a Ret. District Evangelist, Clifton, New Jersey: *The Grandma Series* helps those in need, inspirational, heartwarming, ends with a beautiful example of how God explains our pain, renews hope, shows us the way, creates miracles. I love this series.

Patricia Robinson, wife of a Ret. Rector, Indiana: 5 star rating: *When God Broke Grandma's Heart*: WONDERFUL INSPIRATIONAL NOVEL, enjoyed this book, well written, Bible references, how to achieve peace of mind and soul.

Rosemarie Schaal, wife of an Ret. Reverend, New York: *Abiding Faith, Hidden Treasure:* Reader develops empathy, feels emotion, hears a battle between scientific and spiritual knowledge. Skillful, detailed, brilliant, vivid, teaches that nothing happens that is not planned by Him.

Colette van Loggerenberg, wife of a Minister, Scottsville Congregation of Pietermaritzberg, South Africa: *Grandma's Little Book of Poetry: The Story of God's Plan of Salvation:* This has to be one of the BEST EVER books that I have read....If you ever get the chance to get one of Helen's novels...READ IT. It's like a fairytale but a TRUE fairytale.....Close your eyes and picture this: Grandma with her hair in a bun, glasses perched delicately on her nose, sitting in a rocking chair and her grandchildren sitting on the floor with BIG eyes hanging onto her every word.....but with a twist!!!!! If you have doubts about PRAYER...read this book. I LOVED IT...thank you!

Debbie Espeland, wife of a Rector, Palm Beach Gardens Congregation, Florida: 5 star rating: *When God Took Grandma Home:* HEARTWARMING! This book touched my heart. It is both heartwarming and very spiritual.

Aletta Venter, wife of a Deacon, Scottsville Congregation, Pietermaritzburg, South Africa: *"Grandma's Little Book of Poetry: The Story of God's Plan of Salvation".* What a learning process for me. Oooh I just **love** the way the angels are telling the story, **very original!** When is mankind ever going to learn? The inhabitant's lesson was to learn of good and evil. And they failed miserably each time. The devil has his agenda, and the inhabitants are the target. They call upon God for help, the angels rejoiced. Great....!!!

Aletta Venter, wife of a Deacon, Pietermaritzburg, South Africa: *"Abiding Faith, Hidden Treasure"* is the deepest and most rewarding novel I have ever read, touched my soul, made me cry, author's understanding of God's work is astounding, opens the mysteries

Lisa Mayo, wife of Minister, Palm Beach Gardens Congregation, Florida: Helen's *Why God Why* series of books gave me a new understanding of my faith. They are informative, so enlightening and in-depth, but in a way that is easily understood!!

Tammera Shelton, M.S. Psychology, Odenton, Maryland: I find *"When God Broke Grandma's Heart"* inspirational, beautifully portrays need to let go of negative events and that despite injustice, no pain is for naught.

Robert W. Rothe, USMC 1970-1976, Nevada: 5 star rating: *When God Broke Grandma's Heart:* Outstanding writer, kept me riveted, an angel sent to help through trying days. Thank you for helping me find peace.

Katharina Leipp, Schopfheim, Germany: This is the first time I have ever heard of a female New Apostolic author and I am very impressed by your articles. I have sent your link to my Shepherd and German friends and would like you to consider advertising in our German *Our Family Magazine.*

Claudine Visagie, South Africa: I'm trying to think of a way to introduce Helen's books and articles to others... especially to our youth. They are life changing!

Rabecca Mukuta Mukato, Lusaka, Zambia, Africa: Speaking on behalf of my Dad, District Elder Mukato, your articles are brilliant because they have changed me! Because of your articles my Dad has less headaches!

Robert Henry Parkes, Pietermaritzburg, South Africa: You are gifted with the verses and writings you do and are so inspiring to others. God is really using you as His special servant. You are really a wonderful person and we thank the Lord for you our sister in faith.

Frank Geores, from Port St. Lucie, Florida: *"When Grandma Chased The Spirits:* beautiful spiritual experience, can see caring nature and loving heart of author, eloquently reveals her love for God and search for truth. Worthy of the Star of Bethlehem rating. Thank you for sharing your magnificent gift.

Ben Lodwick, Avid Reader., from Brookfield, Wisconsin: Wow! An eye opener about God's plan of salvation, and why bad things happen to good people. Reminds me of Jim LaHaye and Jerry B. Jenkins "Left Behind Series". MUST READ!"

Dr. Walter Forman From North Palm Beach, Florida: *Grandma's Little Book of Poetry: The Story of God's Plan of Salvation:* a "wonderful book about success and failure in life. All Helen's novels are wonderful, a balm for the soul and an education to the seeker."

Susan Day, From Jupiter, Florida: *Abiding Faith, Hidden Treasure* : I hated to put it down, couldn't wait to pick it up, read all Helen's books, proves every point, shows what to do through God's words. I am 90 and Helen's books have helped me call on God.

Georgette Rothe, From Fort Piece, Florida: *Abiding Faith, Hidden Treasure* was more than I expected; a Biblical course making you re-evaluate your beliefs, enjoyed the journey very much.

Fred D'Alauro, from Palm Beach Shores, Florida: Internet 5 star rating: *When God Took Grandma Home:* Remarkable! Inspirational, moving. Fascinating storyteller with a real message.

Debra Forman, Chester, New York. Internet 5 star rating: *When God Broke Grandma's Heart:* Written from the heart, shares the strong beliefs that shelters us in times of need, courage captivates the reader. Thank you.

Anonymous: Internet 5 star rating: *When God Broke Grandma's Heart:* WHEN LIFE GETS YOU DOWN, PICK THIS BOOK UP, it wrapped its arms around me. A wonderful read. Congratulations on an inspiring work.

A reviewer, a reader in Kentucky: Internet 5 star rating: *When God Broke Grandma's Heart:* Well written, heartwarming, overcoming heartbreak through God, touches your heart. A worthwhile read for all generations.

A reader: Internet 5 star rating: *When God Broke Grandma's Heart:* a must read for all generations. FANTASTIC!

A reviewer Internet 5 star rating: *When God Took Grandma Home:* Moves you, captivating.

A reviewer, a Kentucky reader: Internet 5 star rating: *When God Took Grandma Home:* MUST READ! Touching story of life's tragedies and how lessons learned from these heartbreaking events can turn into blessings.

Description of the Characters in the Novels By Helen Glowacki

Grandma: Grandma's life was filled with sibling betrayal and marital abuse. Her love of God, home remedies and famous boxing stance touches the heart.

Sarah: Sarah helps Grandma write her journal, learns about God's plan of salvation and the enemy who wants to harm her. She carries on Grandma's legacy of faith.

Matt: Matt, Sarah's husband, has a rock-like faith but when he loses a loved one, struggles with his anger with God, until he has a miraculous experience of faith.

Paul: Paul is Matt's older brother who earned a Captain's license for a seagoing tugboat. His faith sustains him despite enduring terrible circumstances.

Mary and Kevin: Mary and Kevin become Matt and Sarah's neighbors and friends. Mary's panic attacks end when God brings a miracle they never thought possible.

Elizabeth: Elizabeth adopts Rebecca, loses her husband twelve years later, is confronted with a potentially deadly illness and searches for Rebecca's birth mother.

Rebecca: Rebecca is Elizabeth daughter and Jayden's friend. Her father's death, the illness her mother faces, and a series of challenges at college almost destroy her.

John: John, a deacon, lost his wife to a debilitating disease, becomes Elizabeth's friend, and helps his daughter and grandson through a difficult divorce.

Jayden: Jayden is John's grandson and becomes Rebecca's friend. He has learned that prayer helps solve problems and he and Rebecca begin to share their faith.

Wade and Ruth: Wade is Jim's boss and friend who adopts two children from Iraq. Ruth is Jayden's mother and John's daughter who struggles to let go of the past.

Joshua and Debbie: Joshua, Sarah's younger brother, was demanding and judgmental until Caleb stepped in. Debbie looks to Joshua's family to be her role models.

Caleb and Ann: Caleb is Sarah and Josh's older brother and the family looks to him as they once looked to Grandma. Ann, Caleb's wife harbors a secret sadness.

Barbara and Jim: Barbara, Matt's sister is also Sarah's close friend. Her husband Jim plays devil's advocate in family debates, and matchmaker for his friend Wade.

Heza and Bara: Heza and Bara endured a suicide bomber attack when Bara was one and one half years old and Heza as she was born. They are adopted by Wade.

Chaldeth: Chaldeth is a fallen angel sent to destroy Grandma's family. He plots to bring great heartache to Rebecca and Jayden and their family to break their faith.

Durk: Durk, abused by a cruel father, is a sophomore at the college Rebecca and Jayden attend. He brings harm to Rebecca and Jayden but Jim gives him a second chance.

Professsor T. Nagorra, and Emils, and Dean Peerca: These tenured professors befriend Durk and engage in activities that bring harm to the students and campus.

Professors Doog and Sendnik, and President Legna: These three share a faith in God, a love for their country, and desire to be role models. They help save the campus.

Richard and Rachel: Richard is a physician for whom Caleb built a house on the property next door to where he and Ann. live. Both couples share godly values and thus became friends.

Joe and Preacher: Both men work for the company which hired Caleb to supervise the construction of a shopping mall. Preacher is always trying to teach Joe what scripture says.

www.ingramcontent.com/pod-product-compliance
Lightning Source LLC
Chambersburg PA
CBHW031106260626
47172CB00001B/240